The Golden Mark

By
Scarlet Darkwood

Chapter One

In the back hallway, Blake McCallahan sat hunched over a pock-marked desk, brooding over some papers he found in a rickety old filing cabinet. This afterthought of a room in his father's comfortable rustic cabin gave him a place for escape so he could prowl and relax in solitude. With any luck, the letter in his hand held a clue for planning his real escape and a way to support it afterward.

"My old man has never said anything about a business he owned years ago," he mumbled.

As a matter of fact, Jared McCallahan didn't talk much about the past at all. Not that Blake asked a whole lot of questions. Like his dad, he was a brooding quiet type who kept his nose to the grind and stayed out of trouble. In the black market, a body had to do that or risk jail time. Worse, one wrong move could land you six feet under.

He'd been a privy to "the biz" since the day he was old enough to understand what "keep this strictly between us" meant. His father had a finger on the pulse of the market, studying the next hottest forbidden commodity that could be bought for a good price and sold at a better one.

Unlike his dad, being king of dark money didn't interest Blake in the least. His current goal: head for the door, make a clean break, never look back. The expansive cabin he called home lay nestled in the hilly lands of Johnson City, Tennessee. If all went as planned, the large nearby cave where the goods were stored would gladly be a distant memory.

Beneath the light of a small desk lamp, he studied a shiny gold-foiled logo bearing the emblem of a crown inside a circle. The words King & McCallahan fell in line beneath. Blake scanned the contents of the letter, quickly noting the high-peaked lettering in the author's hand-signed signature at the bottom.

Something about a business ending. Elite gifts and fine curiosities. Puzzled, Blake sat back and glanced at the date. His eyebrows shot up. What kind of gig was this? The business existed years before he was born.

He knew one thing already. Gifts and curiosities peaked his interest. What would it be like to own a business never having to look over your shoulder? His gaze glossed over the words. Statements about interests and actions not being true to the original goal.

Trust between partners dwindling. Yada yada. Declarations that it would be best to accept the buyout offer or loose shareholder power. Worse, suffer legal action. Blah, blah, blah. Just as he turned his eye to the name of the person who sent the letter, the sheet of paper disappeared from his hand.

"What do you think you're doing, son?" Jared McCallahan whisked the document away, jerking up the envelope as well. He stuffed the letter back in place and tucked everything inside a pocket of his discolored jeans.

"Why have you kept a letter that old, and who wanted to buy you out, or else?" Blake sat back in the wobbly desk chair, quickly steadying himself before he and the chair toppled over.

Jared grimaced and shook his head. "Was a long time ago. I thought I'd tossed that letter." He stared into his son's face. "You've been spending an awful lot of time back here."

"Have we talked about adding fine gifts and curiosities to our inventory? I could run the division." Blake's lips played into a mischievous smile. He scooted closer to the desk, resting his elbows on the surface. "I'll even pick all the goodies. What do think?"

"You're full of wisecracks." Jared answered. "What happened then means nothing now."

"Who was the business partner, and is he the reason for what you do today?" Blake angled his head sideways a little.

"Too many questions, boy." Jared grinned. "Get out from behind that infernal desk and let's celebrate. You're twenty-one today."

"Give me a few more minutes, Dad. I need to straighten up a few more things." Blake watched his father nod and leave the room. He thought back to the letter. Seemed like the King fellow was too much on the up-and-up for his father.

Sounds of voices grew louder, trickling underneath the oak door. Blake sucked in his breath and filed several small stacks of paper in another filing cabinet. "What's this?" he muttered. A folder in the top drawer bulged with something, and it wasn't papers. His interest turned immediately on a gold-tone box he pulled out.

He tried opening it. Nothing. He shook it. Thought he heard a light rustling inside. Turning the box over, he wrinkled his brow. The gold surface had dimmed with age. Did it have anything to do with the letter Jared had swiped away? The key, where ever it was, must be tiny.

Blake ran his finger over the lock's facing. He'd have to find a better time to ask about the mysterious discovery. Breaking away from his intrigue, he stuffed the box back in its original place.

Time to go out and face the crowd. That's what it sounded like outside the office. Had his dad planned something big?

"About time you got here. We were about to form a search party." Jared grinned when Blake stepped into the roomy den.

It smelled of old leather, wood, and Cuban cigars. Many a party had been held in this house, with forbidden liquors, smokes, and the richest food money could buy. Tonight, the visitors consisted of men and women holding fine crystal glasses of burgundy.

Blake knew each pop of a cork cost at least a minimum of a hundred dollars. He waved to Shorty, a staff member tending bar at the far end of the room.

"Happy Birthday!" Eileen spoke up. Her eyes lit up as much as the smile spread across her face.

"Thanks." Blake nodded and walked toward her, hugging her slender body close to his.

She and Jared had been a couple for many years. She'd been more of a mother to him than his real one, who had skipped out two years after he was born. The subject of Blake's biological mom never came up much. His dad did a pretty good job of stepping up and giving lots of love and attention when he could, considering his line of work.

"You did this for me?" Blake gazed around the room, smiling. On a large table he viewed a tasty gargantuan cake fashioned in the shape of an armadillo. He hoped that the underneath consisted of his favorite flavor, red velvet cake.

Jared handed his son a glass of wine. "Drink up buddy. You're becoming more of a man every year." He slapped his son affectionately on the back.

"We wanted to hire a stripper but couldn't get anybody to come way out here." Shorty laughed. "I think we scare people."

Everyone else chuckled.

"You're a motley crew. I wouldn't come out here, either." Blake teased back.

"You really need a girl." Eileen ruffled his neatly cropped brown hair. "You're too cute to be alone."

"Someday. Maybe." Blake surveyed the woman standing next to his dad.

For an older couple, they presented a rather stunning picture of fine looks and good taste.

"My aunt's cousin's niece is nice I hear. If you can stand a bossy chick with a wart on her nose." Shorty grinned his biggest. "But she's good where it counts, and you can always cut out the lights." His face sobered while his eyes turned upward to one side.

The room filled with laughter.

"Who's going to serenade the birthday boy?" Eileen asked. She turned and viewed the guests.

Four men leaned their heads toward each other and nodded.

"Shorty, get your harmonica," said one of the men.

Shorty's smile widened. He stepped out from the bar. From inside his pocket he pulled out a small instrument. Blake eyed the flash of silver with curiosity.

"Ready on three," said Shorty, standing a few feet from the men. He blew out a long monotone strain from the harmonica. The men hummed in unison, tuning their vocal pitch. "One. Two. Three."

The men broke out in a Barbershop Quartet-style rendition of "He's a Jolly Good Fellow" followed by "Ugly Girl." The last song was Shorty's choice. "I couldn't resist," he said. "Birthday boys always need advice, about marriage, and we thought that one was pretty good. If your old lady's not a looker, you won't mind if she goes lookin'. Know what I mean?"

Blake chuckled, clapping his hands. "That was great, guys. Whoo-hoo." He let out a sharp whistle of approval.

"I hire only the best," said Jared, pointing at his cohorts.

"We jacked up the rate just for him." One of the men winked in Blake's direction.

Eileen and Blake laughed.

"Cake time. First piece goes to our guest of honor." Shorty headed toward the table. He placed the end of a cake knife in Blake's hand. "Step right up, young man." He pointed to the armadillo. "May I recommend the end. There's nothing like a fine piece of tail."

The men broke out in a chorus of guffaws. Eileen and the women stifled giggles.

"Is that all you think about?" Jared laughed and sipped some of his wine. "You'll ruin him."

Shorty looked up from the cake. "He knows I'm just kidding." Glancing back at Blake, he added in a loud voice, "seriously, nice tail is where it's at. Not all of where it's at, but you know what I mean."

"You're not right, man." Black snickered.

"Just remember. My aunt's cousin's niece." Shorty put a hand to his ear, mimicking a telephone receiver. "Call me," he mouthed.

Blake shook his head, chuckling. He stood back and viewed the people as they served themselves cake and filled small china plates with caviar, specialty cut breads, cheese, and meats.

Hard to believe these same people who appeared harmless and ordinary spent their work hours cutting deals, striking bargains, and outsmarting the law. He swore some of the men in the crowd may have killed a person or two. Eileen had stationed herself with an intimate group of ladies in a far corner. Jared and several of the men chatted at the bar.

Three younger men, closer to Blake's age, sat on a leather sofa, drinking and making small-talk. They made up the cast of latest newbies on his dad's team. He always wondered how people struck up an interest in selling off-limit goods.

There had to be a daredevil streak in everyone present. That and pure greed. And heartlessness on some level. Some of what his dad sold sent his nerves on edge.

What was his streak? The more he thought about it, Blake hadn't quite put his finger on it. He understood business. Jared let him decide on the next go-to item several times, and he'd been right. The satisfaction had been bittersweet.

"What are you thinking about so hard?" One of the men on the sofa spoke out.

Blake broke his reverie. He headed their way and sat in a nearby chair within talking distance. "Little bit of this. Little bit of that."

"We were talking about setting up a team of sports bookies. Lots of money in it. Wanna join in?"

"No. I don't want in. Thanks." Blake's words left his mouth before he barely processed the question.

They all sat and stared at him, stunned.

"I mean, I'm not big into sports. There's lots of money in betting, though. Maybe if you pool your winnings, you might open up a fine casino." He blinked a few times. "Worth a shot."

The men considered his words.

"Great idea. Might work." One of the men nodded and grinned.

"You into anything special, Blake?" Another man got up from the sofa and pulled up an extra chair that had been set out for the guests. "We kinda talk amongst ourselves, if you haven't noticed already." The man punched Blake's arm and look in the direction of his pals. "We wonder how happy you really are. You don't seem happy at times."

"Do you like working with your dad?" asked another man.

The remaining men found spare chairs and gathered near Blake.

"Dad's great. What's not to like?"

"You with a woman?" Another man chimed in. "We never see you with one or hear you talk about going out."

"Waiting for the right one," said Blake. The men pulled back, shifting in their seats. If a conversation could head south at warp speed, this one was doing a fine job. "Great talking to you guys. I'm going to mix and mingle." He got up from his chair. "Keep working on the bookie deal. And the casino. Possibilities are endless. Don't forget it."

Blake knew the men would have a field day tomorrow, whispering behind his back. He spotted his dad at the bar staring in his direction. Had he heard snatches of the conversation? Something in the stare bothered him. His face wore the same expression of disapproval he sometimes displayed to Blake when something didn't go his way.

Jared pushed himself away from the bar and walked toward his son. "You having a good time? Those guys over there are great. Promising." He leaned his head lightly toward the small group.

"They're full of ideas. They'll be the best wheelers and dealers on the force. I know it." Blake forced a smile. His dad was leading up to something. His gut clenched.

"You're full of ideas yourself. I'll bet you can wheel and deal with the best of them. What breaks my heart is you don't seem intent on doing it for your old man." Jared rested his hand on Blake's shoulder.

The two stood in silence for several seconds.

"Let's go outside a minute, get some fresh air." Jared led the way out a side door leading onto a small porch. The two walked down a few wooden steps, landing on soft green grass. They made their way to a split rail fence separating the house from a field.

The Tennessee sun glowed neon orange, hanging on the edge of a fading silvery gray sky. The smell of dirt and trees filled the air. First sounds of crickets started an orchestra for the oncoming night. Blake took in the view.

He loved the eastern region, filled with colorful mountains, rolling meadows, rivers, and streams. He didn't need to stay here with his dad to enjoy it all, either. Another world waited out there for him, and spirit sirens called his name. Given a chance, he'd slip into the dark and never be seen again.

"What do you want for your birthday?" Jared's soft voice broke the silence.

"Huh? You don't have to get me anything." Blake turned and viewed his father.

"You didn't answer my question."

Blake shook his head, staring off toward the mountains.

The crickets joined in numbers, chirping louder. A swift breeze blew, disappearing in seconds.

"I want you out by the end of the week. You hear me?" Jared finished off the rest of his wine.

Shocked, Blake stared, watching the silhouette of his father slip across the grass, back inside the house.

Jared's statement unlocked a torrent of emotion. Blake didn't know whether to shout for joy or scream in fear. Fear, only because he hadn't come with the other part of his plan. What would he do now that he didn't have his father's business for support?

The bookie idea suddenly seemed like a good one. Was it too late to join the gaggle of dudes who had accosted him from the sofa?

"You okay?"

Blake jumped at the touch. Eileen had come up from behind, wrapping an arm around him. "You know he loves you." She wiped the side of her eye. "Your dad. He loves you. That was the hardest thing he's ever had to say in his life." Her voice cracked.

"I'm glad he said it." Blake forced a chuckle. "Saved me the trouble of telling him myself."

Eileen nodded, sniffling. She hugged Blake tighter.

"I won't lie. The only thing that worries me is finding new work."

"You've got all kinds of connections, sweetie. The people who work with your dad know . . . what do you call them? Honest people." She laughed and kissed the side of his head. "We can point you in the right direction. But if you want to really go your own way, get on the internet and look under all the job sites."

"I've done some of that already. The thing that stumps me is how do I tell them about . . .? Blake pointed back toward the house. "All of them? I can't lie on a resumé."

"We'll take care of that for you. Trust me, we can finagle some company names, owners, anything that you'll need for references. Remember, sweetheart. All you want is one good first job, and the world is at your feet."

Blake smiled at Eileen. The moon had come out. Her beauty held him under a brief spell. The allure of her mesmerized him. No, he didn't have the hots for his father's girlfriend. But if he could find a woman like Eileen, he would finally believe he had the world by the tail.

"Come back in with me and get some more cake and food. The guys want to chat with you."

Eileen and Blake walked back to the house. He entered a different man than when he left. A few magic words, and the spell had been broken. Next week he would no longer walk in his father's shadow, doing work he hated and never believed in. No more worrying about a deal going bad.

He'd strike out on his own, maybe make a name for himself. Retail he liked. Honest retail he liked even better. Did the King of King & McCallahan still exist? Blake wanted nothing more than to hear about the curiosities his dad once peddled. Did his dad create any of them? What did the gold-tone box hold?

When he settled in among the guests, he didn't see his father anywhere around.

Chapter Two

Jared stood with his son next to the filing cabinet where the old letter had been found the night of the birthday party. He lifted some folders and pulled out an eel-skin wallet resting beneath them on the bottom. "I've kept this hidden for a while. Can't remember where I got it or who gave it to me, but it's yours now."

Blake watched, noting the tight look on his father's face. He dared ask the question he hadn't since the night Jared made his order clear. "You mad at me?"

Jared turned toward his son, rubbing his finger against Blake's cheek. "I'm disappointed, but I'm not mad. I want you happy more than anything. More than keeping you here with me. They say if you love something, let it go. Isn't that right?"

"I'll come home every once in a while. That's still allowed, isn't it?"

"You'll always be welcome back home, son. I'd never turn you away. That you can bank on." Jared smiled. A thoughtful expression filled his eyes. "Speaking of banks, I made a trip to one yesterday. Put this in that fancy wallet of yours." He handed over a thick roll of hundred-dollar-bills.

Blake put them away like his dad instructed.

"Should get you started until you find something. I suggest you find work quick, because that won't get you far these days." He winked at his son.

"Any suggestions on who I can talk to? You know what they say, knowing people who know people are the best for getting jobs." Blake felt rather proud of himself for sounding somewhat legit. He could let his guard down with Eileen, but he had to save face with Jared.

"I think Shorty would be a good one to talk to. Since he's full of such good advice and nonsense." Jared smiled. "Besides, he wants to say bye. He really likes you, and he's one of my best men."

"Will do, Dad."

"There's one other thing I want you to have." Jared walked toward another filing cabinet.

Blake's pulse quickened. The cabinet was the same where he had spied the gold-tone box. To his surprise, his dad pulled it out.

"You see this?" asked Jared. "Take it with you. Be very careful and don't lose it. One day you'll know why."

"One day? How do I open this? I couldn't find the key."

"I know you've tried like hell." Jared grinned. "I'm not about to tell you. Truth is, I'm not sure where I put the key. Ask Shorty to give you some lock-picking lessons."

"Can you give me a hint what's inside?" Blake took the box from his dad and shook it like he did before.

"No." Jared gazed at his son. "I'm asking that you only open that box on one condition."

Blake wrinkled his brow.

"Open that box on the day you're married. Promise me that one thing. And there's one other catch. I'm giving you five years to do it, or the whole deal is null and void. Make sure you love her as much as I love Eileen."

"Five years? Married? But you and Eileen are not . . ." Blake blurted out.

Jared frowned.

"Yeah, sure, Dad. If it's that important to you. Five years? Really?"

"Just do what I say. Make me the promise."

Blake held out his hand for a gentleman's handshake. "I promise I'll only open the box the day I marry the love of my life. In five years." He grinned.

"Good." Jared glanced at his watch. I gotta run. Go talk to Shorty."

***

From his hometown of Johnson City, Blake hopped in his Nissan 350Z Touring and headed south. The Southern part of Tennessee didn't disappoint. At least Blake thought so as he drove to the town of Pigeon Forge. Fields rose and dipped, carpeted in rich green. Mountains stood solid and stubborn against a blue sky.

Jared and a tearful Eileen had watched as he drove out of sight. It had been smooth riding on the interstate, but when he reached Sevierville, the traffic slowed a bit. At a red light, he pulled out a slip of paper from his wallet. Calin Shepherd. Shorty had scrawled the name in blue ink. "Look for him, and he'll set you up." That's all his dad's best cohort said.

Blake had no idea where to start, nor where Calin Shepherd could be found. Here he was, all ready and eager. And nowhere to go. Shorty offered only a couple of clues. "Check Pigeon Forge or Gatlinburg," he said.

At least Shorty limited his choices to two possible towns. They were next to each other, which was a good thing in a vast, limited way. He kept driving straight. The traffic turned into a hectic mess once he reached Pigeon Forge. Tourist season was in full swing. Cars lined the parking lots. People filled the buildings. An amusement park, hotels, shopping. Everything anybody could want.

If he wanted to indulge in retail of any kind, he'd hit the jackpot in this town. Gatlinburg and the artisan community were just as good. On impulse, he turned down a side road when he reached another traffic light. A large building stood on the left. Cobbly Nob Mill Family Restaurant.

Perfect. Blake parked the car in an empty space in the back. Seemed like a popular place. People came and went. As he locked the car door, he sniffed. A faint smell of food hit his nose. His stomach growled. Time for a good hot meal and people who might help solve a mystery.

He pushed his way into the rustic building and landed a seat by a window with a view of a river rushing through the forest. The sight of it put him immediately at ease.

"What can I get for ya?" A plump waitress with big teeth and wearing an apron stood beside Blake, holding her pencil poised over an order book.

"I'll go for the meatloaf, carrots, and mashed potatoes." He smiled and handed back the menu.

"What'll ya have to drink, hon?" She managed a smile between chewing her gum.

"Coffee and water."

"I'll have everything out, shortly."

"Miss," said Blake, reaching out and touching her arm, "do you happen to know a Calin Shepherd who might live around here?"

The lady chewed her gum faster than ever. She scratched her messy mop of hair, thinking. "Never heard of him. Is he somebody big I should know about?"

"Just asking. A friend told me I could find him here in Pigeon Forge or Gatlinburg."

"Don't know, hon. Let me get your order in."

Blake turned his attention to the river. Over time, flowing currents had smoothed the surface of the stones, polishing them to a fine sheen.

He wanted his own place with a view just like this. Lots of woods with a river running through. He also wanted a woman to enjoy it with him. The guys at his birthday party struck a nerve. One day he'd have a woman who outshined anybody they brought home.

Twenty minutes passed. Where was his meal? The waitress at least brought him the coffee and water fast.

"You looking for me?" A portly man wearing a hat stood next to Blake.

"Excuse me?"

"I'm Calin Shepherd. My friend said you were looking for me. Didn't know who you were or where you came from. Thought I'd better come look."

"The girl who's waiting on me said she didn't know you." Blake motioned for Calin to sit down.

He pulled out the vacant chair and dropped down with a huff. "My friend owns this place. She must have told him. He called me."

"I got it." Blake smiled. "Can I buy you something to eat? Maybe we can talk."

The meals came. Blake brought Calin up to speed on why he'd ended up in a small yet hopping town like Pigeon Forge. He left out the black market aspect, choosing to keep the conversation vague and light. More along the lines of trying to break away from a family business and find his own path.

The older gentleman sat back in his chair, sipping coffee and eyeing Blake. "I know the feeling. When it's time to go, it's time to go. I retired early. It was time to get out of the rat race. Got me a small farm and some animals. Like 'em better than people." He let out a laugh.

"Don't disagree with you there. I'm more of a loner by nature." Blake liked the man. He seemed friendly enough. "I'm wanting to branch out on my own, see if I can find a line of work I like. Shorty told me you could help."

"My nephew? He's a mess, that one." Calin shook his head. "Smart kid, though. I don't tell the other relatives, but he's my favorite."

"He's my dad's favorite too," said Blake, smiling.

"What kind of work are you wanting? I'm a simple farmer now. More of a gentleman farmer, if you know what I mean."

"Do you know anyone who works retail, would like someone to help manage their business?"

Calin scratched his head. "I wasn't in retail. Worked in public utilities. My investments got me my farm." He looked at Blake over his coffee cup. "You schooled in anything? Have a degree from some schmancy college?

"No. I went to a local college about a year and quit. Felt like my family could teach me better than a teacher who'd never owned a business. We've sold goods and services for years. We go where the market takes us."

"Gotta follow the market." Calin said. He placed his cup on the table. "But if you don't have a degree or something special to offer, it's going to be hard finding work. At least something that pays a decent salary."

Blake sat back in his chair. A small wave of defeat crept over him, but he vowed the feeling wouldn't crush his spirits. It seemed his family and their cronies had made extra sure his venture turned into a living hell. He'd die before returning home with his tail between his legs.

"Look, I'm not sure why my nephew thought I could line you up with work, but I'll suggest something. Come to my place. Got an extra room in the house. No wife, so there'll be no fuss. Help me with the farming. It's beginning to get a little out of control for one person."

An interesting suggestion. Blake thought about it. He'd not dealt with outdoorsy work. Ever. He may have been born and reared in a Southern rural town, but his lifestyle fit more of the city boy type.

"I don't know how useful I'll be. Never did any farming in my life. Know nothing about it."

"If you can follow directions, we're good. You may not know a lick about country work now, but that'll change." Calin forked some food in his mouth, watching the young man fidget across the table.

Blake shook his head and stared down at his plate.

"Son, if you can do better than my offer, have at it. You'll have nothing but my blessing. And my admiration for being such a gutsy fellow. But I'm telling you, stepping away from a family business where you called the shots may be harder than you think. Especially if you don't have something better or a hot lead to replace it."

Never in his wildest dreams did Blake foresee his occupational path turning to agriculture. At once, he sensed a bit of hypocrisy. He'd always looked down his nose at people who led more humble lives. He saw them as simple, sometimes not the brightest bunch on the planet.

Now his high-falutin attitude had come home to bite him in the ass. He didn't know how to start tractors or what animals ate. Didn't know anything about planting crops. He'd vaguely heard of crop rotation but knew nothing of what it meant. Had Calin rotated crops? How many animals did one man have?

"I'll do it." Blake let out a hot breath, emptying his lungs. "If you can teach a newbie, I'll do my best to be of some use."

Calin answered, "You'll do better than you think." He sat up straight and leaned over a little on the table. "Let me see your hands. Go on, hold 'em out."

Blake looked around, embarrassed.

"Nobody's looking at us." Calin laughed. He took the young man's hands in his and let out a soft whistle. "You're a softie. Anybody ever tell you that?"

"No. But I'm sure the guys at work had other names they used behind my back. You know how people respect and love their bosses." Blake grinned.

"Had plenty of names for mine. They were lucky I didn't use them to their faces, but a man's gotta eat. You know?"

"Kind of works that way."

The two men spent a few moments in silence finishing their meals. The waitress returned with the ticket.

"I'll buy," said Calin. "We haven't talked about your so-called salary, yet." The older man closed up some bills in the plastic receipt folder and placed it back on the table. "Let's get out of here. Where did you park?"

Blake led the way back to his car. People still drove in to the restaurant. The lot didn't look any emptier than when he'd arrived.

"What did you bring from home? Let me see."

"Only what filled my bag." Blake unlocked the car and unzipped the duffle bag.

Calin squinted as he ran his hands through some clothing and a small bag of toiletries. "That all you brought? You sure packed light."

"Planned on buying everything when I got here, depending on what the new job required."

"Your new job requires a trip to Walmart. You don't have one thing in that bag fit to wear on a farm." Calin looked around, thinking. "Let's shop now while we're in town. My truck's parked over there." He pointed in the direction of a worn vehicle that had seen better days.

"That's my running around, hauling truck. I have a nicer one if I'm going someplace fancy or need to do a better job impressing someone. Didn't know you, so I figured it didn't matter."

The rigs Blake had ridden in back home were fine, shiny vehicles fully loaded with all the gadgets and gizmos available. Seats were usually leather, and the beds fitted with a hard cover so nobody could see what had been hidden as it made a path from point A to point B.

"Got any money with you?" Calin strapped himself into the driver's seat.

Blake nodded. The truck had a musty smell collected from everything his new boss had toted in the back or placed on the passenger's side.

"I can buy and take it out of your salary, or you can do it. Your call." Calin turned the truck on the main road in the direction of Sevierville.

"Do you mind telling me what kind of salary you're thinking of?" Blake couldn't keep quiet on the subject any longer.

"Let's see," said Calin. "You're staying at my place, so there's no rent. Room's clean and furnished, so no money for furniture. Feeding two is not much more than feeding one. I'll buy the groceries, pay the bills. That's it." He gazed out the windshield, slowing at a stoplight. "I'd say fifteen-hundred dollars a month."

Fifty dollars a day. Blake said nothing, keeping his eyes on the road. It might pay for gas, a few extras. Not much left for anything else. "Sounds good," he said to Calin.

The Walmart trip ended up being short and sweet, much to Blake's relief. He shopped far and wide for his clothes, and they usually came from name-brand stores. The crowd didn't excite him any better. He and Calin headed toward the men's wear, pulled out jeans, simple cotton shirts, socks, and a pair of boots. The cowboy hat topped it all.

"You'll need something to keep the sun from burning your head to a crisp," said Calin. He also picked up some bandanas. "You might want something around your head when you get sweaty."

"It's all good. Whatever you think I'll need." Blake didn't balk at anything. His new boss didn't look like the spendthrift type.

"By the way, did you drive your own car?"

"It's all mine."

Calin chuckled. "Should have known when I saw a fancy set of wheels. Let's get on back."

***

It didn't take long before the men traded the hectic streets of Pigeon Forge for calm roads leading to the outskirts of town. Several miles later, they reached rural countryside. Blake followed Calin but turned on his GPS just in case. Farm work or not, things looked a little better after having met Shorty's uncle.

Calin turn his truck down a dirt drive. Only a mailbox with his last name and street number marked on the outside. Blake liked the look of everything already. Open rolling hills and fields lined both sides of the drive. As they drove farther along, pastureland turned into woods with trees shadowing the road.

How far was Calin's house, and did the woods open onto another field? Minutes later, he parked his car in the vacant space under a two-car overhang. The "good" truck had to be parked in the outbuilding he saw by the carport. Upon viewing the house, he liked the grandeur it possessed.

Built in the old farmhouse-style of an earlier era, the architecture showed a white streamlined, two-story framework with matching rooflines and columns in front. Its antiquity showed in the wood and the window framing.

Acres of green spilled out from behind the house. White fencing bordered off the surrounding woods. A bright red barn shone in the distance. Blake viewed the dots of black, brown, and white with some trepidation. He'd have to deal with what looked like cows, horses, and sheep. Did he just hear the bleating of some goats?

"Got me some pigs, too." Calin had sidled up to Blake.

"You got quite a place, Mr. Shepherd."

"Wouldn't have it any other way. This old house belonged to a family for generations. Bought it from their grandson. Promised him I'd take care of it and not sell the land off to some scheming developer. I aim to keep my word. You can take that to the bank." Calin pat Blake on the back and escorted him inside.

The spare room turned out to be one of two others, besides the master bedroom belonging to Calin. Spotless in every way and comfortable. Blake unpacked his belongings, placing them in the closet. Other items went into an antique dresser fitted with an oval mirror. A simple wooden chair sat in front of it.

Nothing like his place back home, but simple and clean. With the money he'd be making, this would have to do.

"Come on down when you get settled. I'll show you around." Calin tapped on the door frame.

"Do I need to change for anything?"

"No. I'll let you have one day free before I put you to work." The older man laughed.

Blake walked with Calin through the pasture, inhaling the growing scent of animal dung. His eyes watered a little. The animals' sizes overwhelmed him. "What exactly do you do with these?" He glanced over at the older man who wore a smile on his face.

"Mostly feed them. I've had a cow or pig slaughtered for my own meat, but I don't do it that much. It's a lot for one person to eat, and I ended up selling a lot of it at the local farmer's market." He laughed. "I took a notion and had my sheep sheared one spring. Tried selling the wool. Lucky for me, I had a woman buy it for her textile business."

"Sounds like you've tried some different ways to make some use out of this farm, other than keeping big pets." Blake smiled, dodging a cow pile.

"I make as much money selling off some of the vegetables that I grow."

"Really?"

"Lot of work, but that's where you come in. One man and a tractor can only do so much."

Calin led the way into the barn. Blake breathed in the strong scent of horses and more manure. Bales of hay lay in neat pile in the loft. A large pile of it lay in one corner, along with a pitchfork. Lots of leather, saddles, bridles, canvas belts and blankets.

"As you can see, I have several stalls for the horses. I have a shed area for the cows over there." Calin walked to the opposite doorway and pointed.

Blake viewed a large roof supported by several beams of wood. A couple of cows stood, shielding themselves temporarily from the sun. The rest grazed in peace.

The two men stepped outside, and Calin led him to another part of the field. "And there are my sheep," said Calin. "I love them." He smiled.

"You have names for them?" Blake stared at the dots of wooly white.

"Not really. If I did more serious farming, I'd probably give them names and put tags in their ears. That sort of thing. But this is all for fun, even if you spend your time caring for them." He looked at Blake. "It's much more rewarding than the old grind."

On the way back to the house, Calin stopped by the enclosure for the pigs. They roamed a sizable area of woods, fenced off from the remaining land. A small shelter had been constructed for their use. One trough had been filled with corn and another with water.

Calin spoke up when he and Blake entered the den, "You have free run of the house. Use the kitchen and this area anytime you want. We can watch TV together. I'll share." He smiled. "You may be my hired hand, but I also consider you a friend. Any buddy of Shorty is a buddy to me. Work days are Monday through Friday, half days Saturdays, and we're off Sunday."

"I can help cook, clean, whatever you need." Blake nodded at Calin.

"That sounds like a fine deal." The older gentleman smiled and headed to his favorite chair.

Blake climbed the stairs to his room. He wanted some alone time. Mixed emotions swirled inside. Part of him saw the new job as a fun challenge. Much of it, he frowned just thinking about the prospects of getting his hands dirty. He simply wasn't used to it. Wasn't sure he wanted to get used to it.

He lay on the bed. The headboard was an antique, high and ornately carved at the top. The mattress, comfortable like the one back home. It dawned on him that nobody from his family had called to check up on him. Not his dad, not Eileen. Not even Shorty. A pang of isolation raced through his body. He resonated with a brief bout of anxiety.

His dad and Eileen could say they loved him, but why hadn't they called to see if he'd made it, asked what he was doing, what is plans were? He pulled out his cell phone and started to press the number to his dad's.

Before pressing the "Call" button, he put the cell phone down. The last thing he wanted was to look desperate. He also knew that leaving a business like his dad's was usually a final deal. Once someone left, no one kept in touch. Why would being the son make a difference?

Blake decided he'd find out soon enough. If they weren't interested, he wouldn't be interested, either. The main streets of Pigeon Forge seemed like fun. Who would he hang out with?

In Johnson City, he had a few friends, did things with his dad and Eileen. All of that had changed in the blink of an eye, it seemed. He was starting over. The prospects thrilled and scared him. Not having an education had put him at a disadvantage in the so-called real world.

Blake got up and pulled the gold-tone box from the dresser drawer. He tried tugging at the top. Did it budge at all? It didn't feel heavy. Maybe it held papers. The money in his wallet added up to five-thousand dollars. Like his dad said, barely enough to get him started anywhere.

But his dad had slipped in some pictures of him and Eileen, Shorty and the gang, and some old photos of him and Blake when both were much younger. He sighed and put them away.

Getting a job was his first concern right now. Getting the girl couldn't be farther from his mind. Luckily, he had five years to do it. Blake shook his head. What an odd request his father had made. But he learned over the years that when you made a promise to Jared McCallahan. You better keep it.

Chapter Three

Blake stared straight into the eyes of a hostile horse. The rope held tightly in his gloved hands slipped when the animal whinnied and jerked up so hard it nearly sent him sailing into the rafters of the barn.

"Whoa, there. Hold 'er tight, boy." Calin peeked around and stared at Blake. He returned to his work with a light grin on his face. "You not ever tended to a horse before?"

"No, Sir." Blake's words came out in a stutter as he gripped the rope harder and pulled down.

The horse stamped in disapproval. It didn't care that a human was treating a large nasty pus-filled wound on one of its back legs.

"Pesky horseflies are a worrisome lot. Tired of 'em biting my horses to death." Calin rattled through his "Vet Box," a plastic toolbox holding all kinds of gauze, ointments, saline solution, bandages, scissors, tongue depressors, and tape. "Hold her good, 'cause this will cause a ruckus."

"Got her, Sir." Blake sucked in his breath and pulled hard. He hoped Calin would finish quickly. His legs trembled with fatigue, and his hands burned with a fiery fury even through thick leather gloves.

The horse let out shrill whinny and bucked again, this time kicking out the affected leg.

"Whoa," cried Calin. He jumped away. "And that's why you always keep to the side. If I'd been behind him, he'd have knocked me plumb to Gatlinburg and back.

Blake managed a chuckle. "There, there, boy. It'll be all right. We'll get you in working order."

"Talk to him real nice. Sometimes that calms them down." Calin nodded in approval and went back to work. "I'll wrap this bandage around his leg, and we'll be done. That cream I put on him stung. But it's best there is for curing fly bites. The vet orders it special for me."

Calin snipped a piece of gauze from a thick roll, wrapped it around the horse's leg, and finished taping it in place. "All done. Take off the rope and he'll wander on out."

The horse did just as the gentlemen said, except for attempting a quick bite on Blake's arm.

"No, you don't." Blake jerked away and backed against a stall post. The horse snorted, turned, and headed out to the field.

"Feisty, that one." Calin put everything back in his box. "I've bred him before. Not with my own, but with other peoples' mares. That's why I hate it when something happens to him."

The two men left the barn. A furry form rushed at them through the grass, heading straight for Blake. "Hey, fella." He bent over and scratched the mutt dog behind the ears. "How are you? Are you a good boy?"

"I think Trigger likes you." Calin called out.

"I like . . . Oh!" Blake gasped and pitched forward, landing face-down in the dirt. "Aw . . . gad!" he groaned.

"Billy, how did you get out?" Calin strode toward the unruly goat and grasped a set of eight-inch horns. "You okay?" he asked Blake.

"I-I think I'm okay." Blake wriggled a little, praying no bones broke. When his mind cleared, he pulled himself up. "That was a hard hit, man." He shook his head. Grass and dirt scattered in all directions. His nose and forehead burned.

Calin's eyes narrowed. "Gotcha a little bit, didn't he? Hopefully nothing hurt other than your pride." He smiled.

The older man made a point. Blake felt equally foolish. His rear end burned too. He chastised himself. The real reason why Billy got out is that he'd forgotten to lock the gate.

"Get on back to the house and take a good long soak. I have some Epsom salts. Come later, your hind end will hurt like all get-out." Calin led the goat back to its enclosure.

Blake made his way back to the house. Upstairs in the bathroom, he frowned when he saw the tear in his jeans. A sizable hole rendered them useless for public wear. The mirror reflected some nasty red scrapes on his forehead and nose. No hiding them. Maybe a light bandage to stop the bloody ooze.

Minutes later, Calin poked his head through the doorway. "Hey, Blake, I'll put these salts on the counter."

"Thanks." Blake closed the door and stripped off his clothes. His butt showed a big bruise with a tiny puncture area. Stiffness had already set in. He ran a generous amount of water into the tub, added the salts, and sank down in hot bliss.

Three weeks on Calin's farm, and he'd already learned how to slop pigs, feed horses, and even milked a couple of goats and cows. Calin taught him how to pasteurize raw, fresh milk on the stove. He had dug up potatoes, pulled off ears of corn and tomatoes, and picked cabbage, carrots, okra. These were a few of the crops Calin had grown. Now he'd been officially attacked by animals.

Working outdoors created a feeling of liberty on some level, but it still didn't change Blake's mind about what he wanted to do in life, whatever it was. He had to figure that out. He had to work on finding Miss Right too. The gold box held him almost spell-bound, and he wanted to know what it contained. But he made a promise. His dad would know if he didn't keep it. Jared always created ways of keeping tabs on people.

An hour later, Blake sat dressed and ready inside his car. The farm failed at providing inspiration for his life's ambition. Time to go where the action was. He started the engine and headed toward Gatlinburg. He'd check out Pigeon Forge in more detail later. He gripped the wheel, winding around the river.

Always the river, sparkling, cold, in a hurry, never stopping. That's how he viewed himself. Something inside pushed him as if time were running out. He'd keep looking, never stopping. The traffic slowed at the main stop light. He edged his way through and found a parking space. Barely.

An eager crowd had set in, lining both sides of the street. When he got out, the vibe in the air hit him like a jolt of electricity. His spirits perked up immediately.

Smells of corn dogs and funnel cakes filled the air. On the main streets and every side road, hotels, restaurants, and shops competed for space. Crowds filed in and out, searching for the next best thing. Country music sounded from shop speakers. Windows teased the eyes with enticing merchandise. Blake's pulse raced.

He walked, dodging people from all sides. Where had moonshine tastings come from? His dad had made boatloads of money from illegal distilleries. He grinned, watching men and women at the tasting counters. A few little sips from those tiny cups would send your head reeling. He knew that much.

Tee-shirts, wood-crafting, candy, fudge, fashion, art. Something for everybody. Did any of this interest him personally? Blake stepped inside a glass-blowing shop. Display cases showed an eye-watering assortment of glittering glass whimsies.

This store interested him more than the others, especially watching a glassblower stretch out a tube several inches before wrapping it in a coil. He wandered out and headed for a wood shop. A man sat behind a counter, etching lines into a piece wood. Blake watched quietly, studying how pieces were made.

Down the street, he found a section paved with cobblestones and bursting with shops at every turn. More of the same. Would his dream fit in Gatlinburg? Could he stand out, create a trinket at an affordable price? He knew long years ago, true artisans and crafters sold their goods here at a fine price. A time when people appreciated unique pieces and didn't bat an eyelash if it cost a little more.

He took to the sidewalks again, watching, listening. The sensation of someone close behind startled him. At once he figured out what happened. A young man had grabbed his wallet and ran, weaving in and out of people, shoving some aside.

"Hey!" Blake yelled and took off running. "Stop that man!"

People turned and looked. Blake pushed his way through, yelling. The faster he ran, so did the thief. Stiff muscles didn't help. Right now, he wanted his wallet and to roast Billy in an open-fire pit. Yards down the street, the thief tripped and fell.

"I'll take that." A man grabbed the thief, splayed on the ground, and jerked him up. "I suggest you run really fast, buddy, before I get the cops. Lucky for you I have this now." He waved the wallet in front of the perpetrator's face and shoved him forward. The young man took off running and turned down an alley.

The older gentleman turned in Blake's direction. "You looking for this?"

Blake stopped running. His chest burned. "That's mine." He took the wallet and placed it in a front pocket of his jeans.

"Saw that no-good-for-nothing running, so I stuck out my leg. Got him, just as I was coming out." The man's eyes trailed upward.

A sign read "The Curious Peddler." Blake glanced through the window and back at the man. "Thanks, buddy. Appreciate it."

"No problem. Glad I could help." The man nodded and disappeared into the crowd.

"That was close," Blake muttered.

Luckily he'd set up an account in one of the local banks in Pigeon Forge. The money he'd brought from home was safe, and his gold box rested in a safe deposit box. He would have still lost fifty dollars if it weren't for the man who stuck his foot out.

Blake chuckled. Maybe he needed to invent a thief-proof wallet. That was one idea he could add to his list of retail items.

***

How could someone lose a herd of sheep? Blake shook his head and swore. He surely didn't leave the gate unlatched again like he did with the goats.

"Sucks to be me, Trigger," said Blake. The dog barked and wagged his tail.

When he came to the far end of the field, he saw the problem. A toppled-over post and the barbed wire with it. Blake let out a huff and looked around Calin's farm as far as his eye could see. His boss was right when he said the farming had become too much for one person.

Fences needed repairs. Some sections required replacing. Other areas needed clearing from underbrush. Calin made sure the animals were fed and cared for, but his garden took a lot of time. The older man had set up a stall at the local Farmer's Market, leaving Blake to make the rounds.

He turned and surveyed the adjoining property. Did Calin own this piece of land too? The bleating of a sheep reached his ears. Blake walked past the fence post and followed the sound to a large pond located lower down in the field. There they were, a herd of fluffy white creatures plucking away at the grass. Their tales flicked, swatting at the flies.

"Trigger, we have to get them back to our place. Don't think they're supposed to be here."

The dog ran toward the sheep. Blake followed. Should he get a horse and help round them up? He glanced back at the barn. Did he remember how to saddle a horse? He fell off the first time he rode one. Calin made him get back on.

"If you don't brush yourself off and try again, you'll be afraid the rest of your life. Can't have that." Calin held the horse while Blake mounted the feisty beast one more time.

"Those your sheep?"

Blake turned his face in the direction of the voice. A man strode toward him. "Oh, boy," he muttered. "I'll have some explaining to do." He headed toward the man, smiling. The smile left his face at once. His eyes widened.

"You the same guy I saw the other day?" The man's eyes narrowed when he came closer.

Blake studied the older gentleman's features. "You got my wallet back for me."

"Name's Aaron Trolle."

"Blake McCallahan."

The two men shook hands.

"You work for Cal?" Aaron asked.

"He just hired me as his first and only worker. I stay at his place."

"Hope you farm better than keeping up with a wallet." Aaron laughed and punched Blake lightly on the arm. "Sorry. I couldn't resist. Wasn't your fault, though."

"Haven't lost it since that time, and I didn't lose it on the way down from Johnson City. I guess my luck ran out."

"Johnson City? You own land up there?"

"No. Getting away from family and starting fresh."

Aaron nodded. "Nice. I remember when I was young, going to school, and trying out life for the first time. Loved it."

"Just trying to figure out what I want to do. That's the tricky part for me, right now." Blake looked over at the grazing herd. "Sorry about the sheep. I was just going to round them up."

"They'll be okay." Aaron waved off Blake's comment. "You in school?"

"No. From what Calin told me, that's a black mark against me." Blake spent a few minutes appraising Aaron about his work experience. Again, minus the nefarious deals.

Aaron stood still, listening. When Blake finished, he asked, "What do you want to do now that you're on your own?"

"Don't know. I've got five-thousand dollars to my name, plus a monthly salary that Calin gives me." Blake stared at the ground a second. "I'm kind of stuck right now." He remembered the letter his dad took away and shared what he learned with Aaron. "I think retail is in my blood. I want unique items I can sell. Not run-of-the-mill junk. I'd like my own business, to tell the truth."

Aaron's eyes lit up. "I may have the answer to all your problems." His lips pulled into a wide smile. "You know the store I came out of?"

Blake nodded. The incident with the wallet cut his time short in Gatlinburg that day. What he barely saw of the shop through the window intrigued him.

"I own that store," Aaron continued. "Me and a couple of my cohorts."

"Yeah?" Blake perked up. "You think I might have a place in your business?" He smiled.

"Absolutely. Good help is hard to find. Keeping it is even worse." He frowned a moment. "I couldn't pay much more than Cal. Besides, many of my students volunteer their time. You mind if I ask how much he pays you?"

Blake told him.

"Nope, can't do better. And I can't give you a place to live, either. So I'd sit tight and hang out here for a while."

"I do have evenings, half Saturdays, and Sundays free, if that means anything." Blake gazed at Aaron.

"How good are you in math?" Aaron asked.

A confused look spread across Blake's face. "I'm okay, I guess. Never had a real problem with it. Why?"

"I teach engineering classes at the university in a town not far from here. I moved out to the country so I could enjoy my free time doing other things I wanted. I could teach you some information that might help you in the future, maybe stimulate your creativity."

Blake considered Aaron's words.

"Does Cal give you a lunch break?"

"About two hours."

"Tell you what, bring me lunch every day, and I'll teach you some things."

"What do you charge?" Blake asked.

"Lunch. Oh, and working some hours in our store on a volunteer basis. We'll work out a schedule that fits yours." Aaron studied Blake's expression. "Need a few days to think about it?"

"Are you seriously saying you can teach me engineering? Outside a classroom?"

"Basic principles, and things I think are beneficial. And I'll let you in on a secret. Learning can be gained anywhere. There's nothing magical about a classroom."

"When would we start?"

"Next week. I'll pick up some text books. Get some notebooks and pencils ready. We'll do this on Mondays, Wednesdays, and Fridays."

"Deal," said Blake. He couldn't believe his luck.

"One other thing, let those poor sheep graze in my field on the days you come. They've about picked poor Cal's to death. Besides, I need some natural lawnmowers." He winked and walked off.

Blake called Trigger. Between the two of them, they rounded up the sheep and ran them back to Calin's enclosure. He spent the remainder of the afternoon repairing the fence bordering the two properties. The only difference, he fashioned a gate so he and the sheep could pass through easily on designated days. Things were starting to look up.

***

The words on the page sent Blake into a near catatonic state. He stared at them, bug-eyed. How did he know what Statics and Dynamics, Energy, Thermodynamics, Kinematics, and Mechanics meant? He picked up another book and saw some of the terminology. Avogadro's number, Boltzmann's constant, Thermal diffusivity, Kinematic viscosity.

He stared at Aaron, open-mouthed.

"Ready to shoe another horse? I have some food scraps from last night. The hogs might like 'em." Aaron grinned and sat back in his chair.

Blake said nothing but blinked several times, glancing from the books to Aaron. Learn what he'd been offered or end up in another career he didn't like.

"You teach this?" Blake asked.

"All the time, almost every day. To lots of people, men and women."

"And they learn what I'm looking at in these books?"

"All the time, every day. Men and women." Aaron took a bite of his sandwich Blake had brought for lunch.

Blake rubbed his lower lip and selected another book. "Principals of Mechanics for Business—Cracking the Code for Searing Your Competition." He looked at the author name. "You wrote this?"

"Sure did. But it's not uncommon for us professors to write books. A lot of us have shown up in journals for the industry. Not your everyday read."

"Does this have to do with your shop in Gatlinburg? Is that why you wrote it?" Blake leafed through the pages.

"Tell you what, buddy, let's get to work on our first lesson. We only have a couple of hours at a time, and there's lots to cover." Aaron grabbed up another book and placed it in front of Blake. "This weekend, you and I will go to the shop. I'll show you around."

"Deal," said Blake. He laid the other books aside and opened a blank notebook.

Aaron presented his lecture, writing on a large whiteboard he'd placed on an easel. Blake took copious notes. When the time nearly ended, Aaron, added, "Read the next three chapters in the book, and we'll continue Wednesday."

Later that night in his bedroom, Blake studied his notes and read one chapter from the textbook. He'd have to finish the other two before he met with Aaron. He reclined on his bed. What had he gotten himself into?

No money. No one to co-sign for a school loan. A strange man suddenly interested in teaching him mumbo jumbo he'd never considered learning. Probably would never have selected in a college curriculum offering. He sighed and started on the second chapter.

***

Aaron turned down an alley off a side rode and parked in one of the spaces behind The Curious Peddler. He unlocked the door to the back entrance. Blake followed. Inside the back room, shelves lined the walls, and an over-sized wooden work table stood in the middle of the floor.

On the table, Blake viewed circuit boards, unidentified mechanical parts, metal and wooden frameworks for various projects Aaron must have had going on. Notebooks, pens, pencils, and a drafting compass added to the disarray. The shelves held reference books, calculators, office supplies, and more of the same that was on the table.

"Looks like you have lots going on."

"This is our work area. We draft ideas and experiment back here." Aaron opened another door, and Blake followed him out onto the main floor of the shop.

Showroom lights lit up the room. Blake's gaze wandered over clocks, fountains, odd boxes, sculptures, and small furniture items. One lady stood behind the register, while her male cohort engrossed himself with merchandising various items.

"Hey, Professor Trolle," said the young lady. "You brought us someone new?"

Aaron smiled and motioned for Blake to follow. "This is Blake. He's my new neighbor, and I just made him swear allegiance to the dark side."

The lady laughed. "Hi, I'm Abby, one of Mr. Trolle's students." She extended a hand to Blake, who accepted it with a warm smile. "Great to have you on board." Abby stared into Blake's eyes a little longer than normal. Blake felt the heat infusing his cheeks. She held onto his hand a little longer than normal too.

"All my students are great, but Abby's my favorite," said Aaron. He spoke the last phrase loud enough to extract a smile from the male's serious look.

"I'm Devon." The young man walked toward the counter and shook Blake's hand, glancing from him to Abby. "Don't listen to him. I'm really the favorite."

"I enjoy all my students," said Aaron, laughing. "Abby and Devon have volunteered to work the shop. I give them extra tutoring and let them try out some of their projects here."

"Do you have any of your projects for sale?" Blake asked.

"See those pots over there?" Abby stepped out from behind the counter, placing her hand on Blake's shoulder and leading him to a shelf by a window. "They deliver water to the plants inside them. If you're away from home, you can use an app I made to place the pots on a timer, or they can shoot out water on demand. Anything you want, really."

She smiled at Blake. His interest piqued. He didn't dislike plants, but he didn't necessarily have a fascination with them, either. He watched as Abby pulled out her phone and demonstrated. He heard a small beep.

"The plants are getting watered as we speak." She nudged him, smiling proudly. "Each pot has a reservoir of water that's used when the sensors are activated."

"I can see how a plant lover would enjoy that." Blake grinned.

Devon walked up and cleared his throat. "Here's what I have." He walked over to a tiny robot and turned it on. "This is the BrushAPet. It has sensors that detect electromagnetic radiation and can determine where your pet is. When it gets close, the brushes on each hand move over the fur." He grinned. "Animals love it."

"You mean animals will actually let that thing go near them?" Blake cocked an eyebrow.

"They have to get used to it through training, so they know there's a reward coming. But, yeah." Devon nodded. "I'll admit that it's better for dogs than cats. And the robot can adjust in height to up to two feet."

"Impressive," said Blake.

Abby asked, "Have you read Mr. Trolle's book, yet?"

"He showed it to me."

"All in good time, guys," said Aaron. "Remember, he's a newbie. You two have been at this for a bit."

"I haven't seen you in class," said Devon. "Are you in another program?"

Blake glanced at Aaron.

"He and I have a different arrangement," answered Aaron. "But he'll be just as knowledgeable, like the two of you, when I'm finished with him."

Abby and Devon exchanged puzzled glances.

"I'll let you get back to work."

When Blake and Aaron reached the work room, Aaron asked, "What do you think? Does it all have the appeal you were looking for?"

"Love the shop. Classy, great ambiance, and unusual merchandise. I didn't look at the prices, though."

"Our wares carry a higher price tag. Even though many of the tourists go for the cheapo t-shirt, funnel cake, or some other souvenir item, we have those customers who appreciate nicer things." He leaned in closer to Blake. "If this store does pretty good, I'm thinking about expanding into multiple locations."

"Do you have a web site?" Blake asked.

"Working on it."

Blake looked around the room and thought about the main floor he'd just seen. His opportunity to be a part of this seemed too good to be true. "I gotta ask you something, Aaron."

The professor squared his shoulders, listening.

"I really appreciate you offering to take me under your wing. And for nothing more than bringing lunch every time we meet."

Aaron nodded.

"Why are you doing this? An education like you're talking about costs a fortune."

"It does. But you are only getting the engineering knowledge without the degree that goes with it. No sitting in formal classes. No electives."

The older man took in a deep breath and moved around the work room, re-arranging items on the table and shelves. His face appeared thoughtful. "Here's the thing, Blake, knowledge is power. And you don't need a fancy degree to have it. Usually.

"Unless you're working for a major corporation and doing special projects that require a license of some sort, you can enjoy everything I'll be teaching you. You'll have an advance view of how most things work. Your mind can take that knowledge and run with it. Create things no one has dreamed of before.

"Forge your own destiny. What I offer gives you a creative advantage." Aaron smiled. "And to answer your question, I make it a point to pick someone every once in a while who needs a break, wants to learn, and still allows me to teach. I love teaching more than anything." He faced Blake head-on. "When I teach, I create the future for mankind. Most of those students are going to make something of their lives, contribute great things to humanity."

Blake stood in awe, soaking in Aaron's words. The passion, conviction of the man's words moved him. "Yeah, I hear you."

"C'mon. Let's get out a bit. See the town, get something to eat. You'll be spending plenty of time in this shop. You'll love it like I do."

As Blake walked out the back door with his new teacher, he believed every word.

Chapter Four

"Look at her go!" Calin laughed, watching a small mechanized contraption zip its way down a row of lettuce. A set of robotic arms reached out, tugged a lettuce head from the ground, and sent it rolling down a small incline into an open receiving box. "How did you come up with that?" He elbowed Blake's arm. "How does it know what to do?"

"Long story short, it has the ability to see solid objects in its path, determine a diameter or width, and pick it up. It has some strong tension in the arms when it meets resistance, so it can pull just about any item from the ground, floor, where ever you put it."

"That would save me a ton of work." Calin watched in awe as the robot picker continued making its way to the end of the row.

"We have one more row to do, and we'll be done," said Blake. "I'll help you wash everything. Then you'll be ready for the next market or any customers who want lettuce."

Calin turned to Blake. "I guess going to the neighbor's place has taught you how to make things like this?" He pointed to the picker.

"Definitely. There's no way I'd ever come up with something like this on my own. He teaches classes, so he's added me to his list. Except I don't go to class. I just go to his place."

"I wondered where you ate lunch sometimes. And it was me thinking you wanted to spend more time with the sheep." Calin laughed again.

"I've got some other projects, if you'd like me to try them out on you." Blake followed Calin behind the machine.

"Try anything you like. If it can help me with work, bring it on."

"Some of this is not exactly the most original, but I came up with the design and the way it works."

Calin patted Blake's shoulder. "There's nothing that's so unique that somebody else hasn't thought of it first. Big farms that grow vegetables for big corporations have gigantic machinery. But what about people like me? You know, farmers who need machines on a small scale. We don't get to enjoy a lot of that. It's costly and a lot of it's just too big."

Blake nodded. "You're right. It's always the little people who get left out."

"Exactly." Calin continued walking. "I think there would be a market for that little ditty you have running right now."

"You think?" Blake looked at his boss.

Calin lifted his hand in a thumbs-up sign.

Blake had spent hours in his bedroom and the work room at The Curious Peddler drawing designs and going through calculations to create the VegePicker. That's what he decided to call this machine. Devon had been helpful. Abby added her suggestions.

Aaron was on the ins with a machine manufacturing organization who supplied the parts for anything he needed. From what he'd just seen with the robotic machine, his calculations and design had worked out perfectly.

The VegePicker could gather more than one type of vegetable. He had designed it with interchangeable parts and an ability to choose the mechanics, depending on what crop you wanted the machine to harvest. The downside, it only did a row at a time. The upside, it ran on an energy source inside the harvester itself. This meant no large tractor or other machine was involved. If he could develop a machine that could pick at least three rows at a time, he'd have an even better winner in a product.

***

"You'll need materials that are weather- and water-resistant." Devon studied the drawings and dimensions in the open notebook Blake had placed on the work table.

"I'll need a timer application too," said Blake. "I want this thing to deliver at certain times. That's what will make it handy."

"What'cha doing?" Abby said, slipping up behind Blake and Devon.

Blake turned around viewing the young woman. He licked his lips. Abby had attracted him the moment he saw her. Slender, pretty face, and a dynamite personality.

"Working on the next best seller," said Blake, smiling.

"If anyone will come up with it, you will." She answered, rubbing his shoulder. "You're smart and a quick study."

Her attention sent a warm rush all over. Blake glanced at Devon, who didn't seem at all amused and definitely not in agreement. Both he and Devon had given Abby the eye more than once. He decided that the only thing between Abby and him, and Devon, was Abby's boyfriend. From the way she talked, soon-to-be fiancé.

"I'm stepping out for lunch," she said. "Blake do you want anything? Devon, I can get you something if you want."

"We'll be fine. Go on," said Devon.

Abby opened the back door and left. Blake watched the hunger in Devon's eyes grow bigger.

"She's pretty," said Blake, breaking the silence.

"Yeah. She is." Devon forced his gaze away from the door and back to the notebook.

"You ever try to win her over from that guy of hers?" Blake stared at his coworker. "It's awfully hard not to."

"She was taken when we both started. I finally gave up." Devon's lips pulled into a wry smile. "But it doesn't stop us guys from trying, does it?" He looked Blake square in the eye.

Blake shook his head. He'd flirted a little with Abby too. No denying it. Her bubbly nature didn't discourage, and she seemed to fancy Blake immediately when he started his first work day at the shop. Devon had watched on, visibly irritated.

But at no time did she ever hint at anything more. Not even a suggestion for drinks or coffee. Not even a suggestion for helping him with his studies. So he'd backed off a bit.

"Since neither of us have managed to win the fair damsel, you want to maybe go for drinks one night after we close?" Blake asked. "We could cry in our beer. And let's face it, if you're like me, all we do is work and study."

Devon's face lit up. "That would be neat. Let's do it."

"Deal." Blake watched Devon leave and return to the showroom floor. He turned back to his notebook and studied his drawings and equations in more detail. Calin would surely like this new project as much as the VegePicker. What farmer wouldn't like it? Again, it saved time and energy, and it could be operated remotely. Again, another winning design.

He spent the next three hours sketching, thinking, re-thinking, and calculating. He'd learned enough from Aaron to have some of the basic calculation equations he needed. Aaron had some spare parts he could tinker with. At eight thirty, he slipped out the back door and headed home.

As he drove, Blake thought about his projects. Could he possibly sell what he'd created at Aaron's? Do a demonstration at a farmer's convention somewhere? Would his head hold all the information Aaron had left to teach?

He felt drained. Months into his new life, and neither Jared, Eileen, nor Shorty had called. With a certain realization, Blake knew he was like others who had left the company. Being the son didn't matter after all.

If memory served him, his dad never had said to call once he got settled in. The acknowledgment filled him with some sadness. Family was supposed to care.

Blake climbed the stairs to his room. The house was dark. From the look of an empty carport when he arrived, Calin had stepped out for the evening. Where would an old man like him go this time of night?

When he went to bed, he crawled between the sheets and thought about Abby some more. He should have hung around Gatlinburg and slipped into one of the bars. Would he ever have the time or energy to be in the vicinity of Miss Right? Abby was out. He and Devon had pretty much admitted defeat. But there were more women out there. One for him.

What would she look like? Would she look like Abby or even prettier? Would she be smart and funny? The more he thought about it, the hornier he got. It had been a good long while since he'd held someone close. He reached between his thighs and wrapped his hand around a stiff throbbing member. With several strokes and an image of Miss Right, he released his pent-up frustration.

***

"Now that's another handy gadget I can live with," said Calin. He gazed down at the swine enclosure, watching the pigs gather at the trough. An automated one that held food in a hopper and could dispense it from the use of an app Blake had placed on Calin's cell phone.

Devon had introduced Blake to the programmer who created all the apps for Aaron's students. The guy had done wonders for the VegePicker. He'd struck another home run on the AutoTrough. Inside Calin's stable, Blake had placed a similar robotic feeder that also delivered hay to the horses.

Blake glanced at Calin. "If you had these automatic machines like I've given you, would you be able to handle this farm alone?"

Calin scratched his head. "It would make my work a lot easier. I could press a button, set a timer, and just let the machine do the work while I do something else. Again, the reason I like these is because someone like me can own them with little fuss and without bigger equipment. Lot of people like me have operations that could benefit from what you've made."

"Think the price is okay? Say, four- to five-thousand dollars apiece?"

"Yes. We pay about that much for one that has to be attached to something. It's still cheaper than buying a tractor."

"Calin, is there anywhere I can market this? Aren't you a member of a farmer's co-op or an organization where I can show this to people like you?"

Calin's face lit up. "I believe there's a way I can help."

Three weeks later Blake made the rounds on Calin's farm. Calin set up all the automated equipment while Blake held a video camera and filmed. He spoke into a wireless microphone, narrating what was going on as each machine moved. Later, he filmed Calin using the phone apps.

These shots would be edited into a set of advertising videos that would go onto several websites belonging to different organizations Calin either knew about or where he belonged as a member. The gentleman had been instrumental in calling, talking to people, and setting up everything. All Blake had to do was film, edit, and upload to the computer.

"You think we got enough? Is there anything we left out?" asked Calin, as he and Blake walked back to the house.

"I think we've got it. Now all I do is put it together."

"We'll see if it works. If you'll let me borrow your laptop, I'll show these clips at the farmer's market. A lot of 'em take a break and wander around. Gotta see what the competition is." He tapped Blake on the arm. "You always have to look out for competition. It'll get you every time. Turn your back one second, and bam! There it goes, taking everything you've dreamed of right out of your hand."

Blake laughed. He thought of Devon in an instant and didn't know exactly why. The young man wasn't any more competition for him than anyone else. Securing patents for his machines had ended worries on that subject. But at times he couldn't shake those jealous eyes. "I hear you, Calin. Can't be too careful these days."

The older man shook his head and sighed.

***

"Lift her up. That's it . . . higher . . . go left . . . too much." Aaron squinted toward the sky.

The afternoon sun shone down in a last valiant blaze of glory. She'd soon succumb to the night. Sheep bleated, running toward Calin's property. Blake worked the drone, moving the controls, trying to gain control over the unruly machine.

"Look out!" yelled Aaron.

One of the sheep jumped and cried out as if it had been shot.

"Damn!" Blake huffed and scowled. He strode toward the drone, Aaron following. "I hope nothing broke. That'll piss me off if it has."

"We have plenty of parts." Aaron grinned. "Try again."

Blake picked up the drone, checked it out, and placed it on a patch of grass. He worked the controls, setting up the machine for take-off. "Let's hope this works."

It lifted off the ground, moving toward the herd of sheep. Blake moved the drone around, lining it up behind a straggler. The sheep took off running toward its buddies. He moved it around to another slow mover, rounding it up in the direction of the herd.

"I think you're getting the hang of your controls, but you still may need to tweak the timing."

"Maybe adjust the weight of this thing. It seems too light, in my opinion."

"Good point," said Aaron, shielding his eyes from the sun. "Use this on a windy day, and you might as well get out the dog and horse. Yeah, making something heavier would definitely be a plus."

"Hey, Aaron, you think maybe adding barking sounds might be good? Something to get them going. You know." Blake lifted his shoulders, casting Aaron a questioning look.

Aaron laughed. "Might be a good idea. Give it a shot. Anything to make it do exactly what you want is always the best. But it seemed okay as is. Just tighten up the controls."

Blake nodded. "I hear you. I'll work on it. When I get this done, it will be another one down. On my project list, that is."

"You are kicking it, buddy." Aaron grinned. "And your lunches are improving. Have you made a robotic cook you haven't told me about?"

"No. But I do cheat, as you can tell." Blake shook his head.

From time to time, he purchased take-out from the Cobbly Nob Mill Family Restaurant, along with pre-made meals from the local grocery store. He placed the warmed-up food in no-spill containers and carried it in a small basket Calin brought him from the farmer's market. "Gettin' all fancy, aren't you?" said Calin, when he brought the basket home. "With what he's teaching you, I guess I'd get fancy too."

"Listen," said Aaron, tapping Blake for attention, "I have a surprise for you this weekend.

***

"What do you think?" Aaron smiled. He motioned toward a space holding models of Blake's projects. Next to them was a laptop showing each video talking about the machines Blake had created, including his beloved drone, the RoundAHerd.

"Wow! That's too cool." Blake stood staring, his eyes shining with emotion.

"Look at you," said Abby. She hugged Blake. "These are fantastic. Have you sold any of them?"

"He's got orders. Several, to be exact," answered Aaron. "I forwarded the link to some of our agricultural sponsors at the university. All the information is included on our website that I've got up and running now. And we have these great brochures." He smiled at Blake. "Proud of you. Fantastic job." He looked at Devon and Abby. "I've never seen anyone absorb information like this guy can."

"Doesn't surprise me one bit," said Abby. "I knew it from the moment he walked in." She hugged Blake again. "Don't forget us little people when you make it really big."

"Aw, no." Blake laughed. "I couldn't have done it without you two."

Devon stood by, his arms crossed.

"Isn't this a great addition to the shop?" Aaron asked, nudging Devon.

"Good. Really good." Devon forced a smile. "Useful too. Can't beat that."

"Agriculture is a great area. Needs to be tapped into more." Aaron adjusted one of the models until he got it in the exact position he wanted.

"All right guys. I'm off. Use your good mojo and make some sales." Aaron headed out the front door.

Blake turned toward his cohorts. "I'll work the front. It's not my day or time, but I'm glad to do it, since I'm here."

"I'm sure the customers will appreciate having you around when they ask about your farm equipment." Devon's face wore an expression of irritation.

Abby scowled at Devon. "Don't you want to work on your project? Blake's giving you some extra time to do that so you can get it on the shelves sooner."

Devon shifted his position. From the look on his face, he regretted firing off.

"That's exactly what I was thinking," said Blake, chiming in. "Go on and get it done. We have some shelves with open spaces."

"Sure." Devon kept his eyes on the floor as he walked to the back room.

"You want to leave early? I can handle this all by myself." Blake turned to Abby.

"Thanks, but I've got plans when the store closes. I'll do some dusting and cleaning up." She smiled and headed toward the supply cabinet.

The shop phone rang.

"Curious Peddler. May I help you?" Blake spoke professionally into the receiver. "You would like to order which model?" He grabbed a pen and notepad.

Abby whirled around, staring at Blake.

"I'll be happy to take your information . . . Yes, you'll really like it. It works just like you saw in the videos." Blake scribbled some lines on the paper. I've got your name and phone number. Can you give me your address?"

A few more lines made their way on the page. "And how will you be paying for this? . . . Yes, we take all the major credit cards . . . Absolutely . . . If there's a problem, we will take care of it . . . Do I know who made it? . . . You're talking to him right now . . . Wonderful, I can run your card if you give me the number. We'll make sure to ship everything when it comes in."

Blake wrote down the number and hung up the phone. He entered the numbers into the payment system. "Sold an AutoTrough. The man said if he liked it, he might purchase a VegePicker."

Abby clapped. "Congratulations. You must be so proud."

In the hallway between the back room and showroom floor, Devon stood, enveloped in dark shadows. He'd heard everything. He grimaced, shook his head, and returned to his project.

Over the next two months, Blake spent some evenings giving sales speeches to various organizations. Some customers came to Calin's farm at his suggestion so they could see the VegePicker, AutoTrough, and RoundAHerd in live action. Orders came in weekly. Even though Blake had to give a royalty percentage to The Curious Peddler, he saw is account with the original five-thousand dollars growing larger by the month.

Once people knew about The Curious Peddler, they came to the shop and talked more with Blake about his machines. Abby had heard his spiel so much that she jumped in and talked if customers asked her about the models. Devon simply pointed them to the laptop and handed them a brochure.

~~End Year One~~

Chapter Five

~~Three Years Later~~

Aaron, Devon, and Abby all ended Happy Birthday in unison, with Aaron adding a few lilting notes at the end. The group had closed up shop early tonight and ended up at Buster & Billy's Roadhouse Bar, a lively joint at the end of the main strip in Gatlinburg.

"Thanks, guys." Blake smiled. "You're the greatest, remembering me on my birthday."

"We just like an excuse to party." Aaron chuckled.

"Hard to believe we've all been together for four years," said Abby. We've had some fun, haven't we?"

"And I can't believe I've taught this guy engineering. In my kitchen." Aaron sat up straight and leaned forward on the table. "I've got something for you. Very special."

"Oh?" Blake took a quick sip of his beer and smiled.

Aaron pulled out an envelope from his pocket. He pushed it toward Blake. "Surprise! I was going to get you a lady popping out of a cake, but rounded up this instead."

Blake squinted, opening the envelope in anticipation. He sped through the text, his eyes opening wide in surprise.

"It's your transcript," said Aaron. "When I made you take exams, I did it for a reason. Those were the same ones I gave my students in class. Talked to the dean. Said he would allow all your so-called classes with me to count as full credits toward a degree. You probably won't need it, but if your life's path requires a degree, you can take the electives and other extra classes required."

Abby's face lit up into a smile. "Aw, Professor Trolle, that is so nice. Very thoughtful."

Aaron beamed. "I may be a nerdy engineer, but I do have a soft side."

Devon nodded with a forced smile. "That's cool, Blake. Much better than slugging it out in class like we had to do."

Abby and Aaron scowled when the words left Devon's mouth.

"Some people need the discipline a structured classroom offers." Aaron turned a pointed gaze at Devon and back at Blake. "I knew when I met this gentleman, I'd found a winner."

"He is a winner," Abby said, nodding. "He's great in the shop. I think our sales have increased because of him."

"So what's the next step now?" Devon piped up, directing his question to Blake. "Still plan on being a farmer, or are you going to get a taste of having your own place and making it bigger in the world?"

The three stared at Blake several seconds.

"You're really expecting me to answer that?" said Blake. "Now? Right here?"

"Why not?" Abby asked. "You may have designed some super fun and handy farm equipment, but you've always said you want to do other things in retail."

"Have you given your life more thought? You're on the brink of having a degree. You have more retail experience. What else do you want to do?" Aaron sat back, waiting for an answer.

Blake thought about it a minute. "I really want my own business and my own team of employees." He grew thoughtful. "And then there's this promise I made to my father."

The group became quiet, turning their attention fully on Blake. He brought them up to speed on the talk he'd had with Jared before he left home.

"That's the strangest bargain I've ever heard a dad make with a son." Aaron shook his head.

"Is he serious about that?" Devon asked. "Do you know what's in that box, even the slightest idea?"

"None. And Dad wouldn't tell me, either." Blake drummed his fingers on the table. "That would be another answer to your question. "I want to settle down and maybe start my own family."

"I don't see a problem with that." Abby spoke up. "If I weren't engaged, I'd consider you." She gazed at Blake. Her face held a sober expression.

Devon's face turned pink. Aaron's eyebrows shot up. Blake smiled.

"Thanks, Abby. Same here. Now that we have confessions out of the way, do I still get an invite to the big day?"

Abby's lips pulled into a big smile. She passed an adoring gaze over a sparkling diamond ring on her finger. "You better come, or I'll drag you out from where ever you are."

"Devon, when are you going to settle down?" Blake looked head on at the young man across the table.

"I'm working on it. I think we've put more time into our studies." Devon fidgeted with the wrapping paper from his straw.

"I'll let you in on a little secret," Blake said. "Old Devon here gets the women. He won't tell you or let on, but when we go out sometimes, all eyes are on him."

"Mmm, nice," said Aaron.

"Aw Blake, I've seen several of them checking you out." Devon grinned.

"I need to think of something, guys. I don't want to be in agriculture, though I've come away with a greater respect for it than before." Blake sighed. "Time for a change, right?"

Aaron held up his mug of beer. Everyone followed. "To changes. May they be the best."

The group clinked glasses.

Blake sat back and thought about his friends. They had really been his family since the day he left home. He and Devon had the strangest friendship. Despite the tension at times, they were decent friends. But he knew his days at Calin's place were numbered. He needed to experience living on his own, making his own way. He had the funds to do it now, the way he wanted it.

Finding a new place wouldn't be too hard. Finding the girl was still the most challenging of all. He had a vague vision of her, one that haunted him in his dreams at night. Would he ever find her?

***

Blake and Devon sat at a bar in Gatlinburg, sucking down beers. Devon had already chugged down eight shots of butterscotch moonshine. His eyes glinted in the low light.

"You must be pretty happy, making all that money." He listed to one side, his words sliding out as he spoke.

"It's helping. Don't make that much where I am now. Mostly because I live there and help Calin. Saves a lot in living expenses, but there's nothing extra. Can't do much else."

Devon caught himself before he fell off his seat. "But you can now. You got money rolling in." He made a rolling action with his hand and slipped off the seat, nearly onto the floor.

"Easy there, buddy." Blake helped his cohort up, hoping the bartender didn't see. Too late.

"Sir, is there someone who will be driving that man home?" The bartender angled his head in Devon's direction.

"We work together. I got him covered." Blake smiled.

"He's way over the limit. He's not getting anything else tonight."

"Not a problem sir. I'll finish up, and I'll take him home."

"Good plan." The bartender nodded and walked over to two cute girls sitting across the bar.

One of the girls looked in Blake and Devon's direction. The beauty of her struck Blake immediately. More than Abby had when he first met her. Thick blonde hair had been twirled into a neat upsweep. A bold pink flower rested neatly clipped on the left side. Down the same side, a long string of tiny floral and beaded pearl dangles framed her face.

He wanted more than ever to whip out his cell phone and ask for a pic. Her red lips sent him into a state of pulsing lust. He could almost feel the succulent flesh on his. Her white lace top rested off her shoulders, revealing creamy ivory skin.

Beneath her neckline, an ornate tattoo of scrolls and flowers splashed across the top area of her chest. In the middle, he caught the outline of a butterfly. She even had a strange tattoo on the right side of her forehead, above the eyebrow. Who was she?

Devon had managed a brief lucid moment, sitting up straight and acting mostly normal, if he didn't move much.

The woman waved. Blake almost waved back but happened to catch Devon's hand slightly raised and moving lightly side to side. He sank back on his stool, watching in disbelief. The beauty across the bar seemed interested in Devon! Someone who was drunk and falling off his stool? No way. An image of the gold box flashed in his mind. Blake let out his breath. Not tonight.

Much to his chagrin, the bartender came toward Devon. "The beautiful lady over there told me to bring you this. But this is really it. No more after this one."

With big smile, Devon took up the drink and held it out toward the woman, nodding his thank you at her. The girl grinned and continued talking to her friend. Blake shook his head and watched his coworker sip down the drink. His only consolation, Devon was really too sloppy drunk to do anything else, even if he wanted to.

"Come on. Let's get you home." Blake stood up and offered a hand.

"I've got it," Devon said in slurred words. "I can handle my liquor just fine. Do it all the time."

"Really? You come here often?" Blake laughed.

"More than you'd think. I don't come out just with you." Devon poked a finger in Blake's chest. He turned and waved at the girl. She smiled and blew him a kiss.

Devon managed to walk out of the bar, casually steadying himself on several tables while he made his way out. "How are you all tonight?" he asked the group at one table. "Have a great night, you guys," he said to another group. And so it went until he was outside.

"I'm dropping you off at your house. Call me tomorrow, and I'll bring you back to the shop." Blake opened his car door. Devon tumbled into the passenger seat.

The streets around Gatlinburg were dark and wound around in one tight coil after another. Houses lined both sides of the street. How Devon and his family ever got out and back home alive, especially at night, amazed Blake. He turned down Gum Stand Road and drove where Devon guided him, praying the instructions were correct.

"It's right here." Devon pointed to a beautiful spacious cabin-style home. The driveway sloped down to the house.

"Nice place." Blake carefully guided the car down in front of three carport doors.

"Yeah," said Devon, trying to focus his bleary eyes on his friend. "We kinda like it too." His face held no expression. He held out his hand. "Listen, buddy, thanks for bringing me home. I'll call you."

"You need help getting inside?"

"Naw."

The way Devon shook his head reminded Blake of how the cows sometimes shook their heads in that slow, aimless way when they were knocking off flies.

Blake stifled a grin. He watched as Devon tripped and stumbled his way to the front door. Someone opened it and let him in.

"Kinda hard when you don't have tables," Blake said out loud. He put the car in gear and prepared for the haul back up the driveway and down treacherous roads. He muttered to himself, "And he still got the girl."

***

"When you get a minute, come back to my office." Aaron had barely poked his head through the workroom door before disappearing.

Blake had barely heard him. He wanted to get the work table and the whole room cleaned up and organized before his scheduled meeting with an apartment landlord. If he liked the unit okay, he'd be giving Calin his notice of resignation. He shelved a few books and made his way down the hall.

At the very end, Blake knocked lightly on the office door.

"Come on in." Aaron's voice rang out. "Have a seat." He pointed to a chair in front of the desk, which held papers scattered in all directions. "Look familiar?" He held out a sheet of paper toward Blake.

The contents on the page piqued his interest. He saw the logo, a crown within a ring, all hot-pressed in gold metallic ink. The only thing missing was the name McCallahan. "You know this guy?" Blake looked up in surprise at Aaron.

"A little. We've met a few times. He's a sharp businessman. Has his fingers in a lot of pies. A healthy bank account too."

Blake read the letter. "Looks like he's wanting some designers for his team."

Aaron motioned for Blake to return the letter. "I want you to talk to him, tell him what you're capable of."

"Does Mr. King know I'm coming? You've talked to him?"

"No. But when you call for an appointment, tell him Aaron Trolle sent you. He'll pay attention. Mark my words." Aaron returned the letter to an envelope and sat back in his chair, studying Blake. "I am only sending you because I have faith in your abilities. You're creative, open to ideas, and you're a quick study. Can't beat that."

"You have a lot of faith." Blake grinned.

"I do. I know you won't disappoint, either." Aaron's face sobered. He sat up and leaned forward on his desk. "If you're free tomorrow, I want to show you something. I'll be surprised if you don't like it."

"Can you give me a hint?" Blake asked

"It kind of goes along with the letter you just read. Sort of, but not really."

"That tells me a lot. Thanks."

"I know. I love to keep my folks guessing. But I think you're going to jump at the opportunity."

Outside the office, Devon hovered close to the door, staying well out of sight, barely breathing so no one would hear him. His heart sank. Always Blake. He seemed to get all the favors, all the lucky breaks. He slipped away and headed to the showroom.

***

Aaron's car hugged the pavement as he and Blake wound their way through Rapid Rivers Road right outside of Gatlinburg. The same road leading them away from the crowd of a bustling strip also led them into another world of enchanted beauty. Surrounding forests towered over them. On the passenger's side Blake's eyes scaled the side of a stone cliff, barely able to see the trees in their full length on top.

The river swirled and rushed, still in a hurry. Moss-covered rocks peeked up from the chilling currents. Blake knew if he dipped a toe in that water, the biting cold would make him grit his teeth.

"I love this scenery," said Aaron. "Never get tired of it. When I drive on this road, it restores my faith in magic. I think if elves and fairies exist, they live here."

Blake lifted his eyebrows and turned an eye on Aaron. He didn't say anything, merely nodding, grinning lightly to himself. Calin's farm had been pretty peaceful, holding a certain charm, but Aaron made a point about Rapid Rivers Road. He felt the magic himself the moment they entered. Something in the ambiance held an ethereal quality, and through the trees, the sunlight cast beams of shimmering white light.

Some wizard must have cast a magic spell once upon a time, and the nature spirits must have topped it with their kisses. Throughout the ages, the forest grew and flourished in all her splendor. What would it be like to live here, see this beauty, immerse yourself in it? As he stared into the depths, he saw the image of her face again.

The woman at the bar. Her face rivaled any enchantress in a fairy tale. The blond swirls of hair. The stream of flowers and pearls. She could have picked any of the tiny blossoms here in these woods. Her red lips, kissable, delectable. If he looked hard enough, prayed hard enough, would she step out from behind the trees, solid, real?

Blake let out a small breath. He had told the landlord he would think about the condo rental he looked at yesterday. Not knowing exactly why, something in his gut told him to hold off. What would he see today?

"Here we are." Aaron had rounded a curve and pulled his car to a stop in front of three rustic buildings. One looked like a cabin, and the other two looked more like work buildings of some kind. Yards away, a river ran through the property.

Aaron placed his hand on Blake's shoulder. "I really hope you'll consider what I'm about to suggest. It will be an opportunity like no other. Let's go take a look."

Both men walked toward the larger of the two plain buildings. Aaron pulled out a key and opened the door. Inside was a large main room. From what Blake discerned, three smaller rooms lined the perimeter. Shelves had been constructed on one side. Beams with hooks hung overhead.

The windows looked like they hadn't been washed in a long time. Sunlight drifted through, showing every crack and dust bundle on the floor. Blake walked around and inspected the other rooms. One was a bathroom. The other two could be used for anything.

"What's the story behind this place, all of it?" Blake looked over at Aaron.

"I'll answer that question after we see the other building and the cabin." Aaron led the way out and walked to the next smaller one a few steps away. He unlocked the door.

This building looked like it had been used for selling retail in its glory days. A checkout counter rested near the door. Behind the glass, Blake saw a few odd pieces of remaining merchandise. An old pipe, some china, and a few sterling silver spoons that had oxidized. The remainder of the room still had some of the displays that had been used. Shelves lined the opposite side of the room, and another set of shelves much lower, covered another side.

"Must have been a nice little shop at one time," said Blake, glancing at Aaron.

"That's exactly what it was. The owners didn't do too bad making a living when they ran this place."

"Owners? What happened to them?"

"Come on. I'll show you the cabin." Aaron turned out of the building, Blake following.

Several yards away stood a wooden structure like the others. A steep tin roof lined the top, and on the porch, two wooden rockers sat on either side of a rather ornate door. Blake stopped and stared at it a moment. The woodwork seemed a little out of place for a cabin crafted of clean-shaven wooden planks. Three stairs led to the porch.

He and Aaron stepped up. The wood felt solid beneath Blake's feet. The more he eyed the cabin, the more he convinced himself that it had been reasonably well-crafted. Some of the techniques used for fastening the planks and beams weren't used much in modern days. Such a shame, because the craftsmanship endured the test of time.

The door squeaked open when Aaron turned the key. Blake stepped inside behind him. His heart melted. The decor and layout looked like it had been modeled from a fairy book story. Polished pine walls, oak floors, and furniture crafted of wood and fine leather. The kitchen held all the modern amenities. When he walked into the bedroom, he knew a fairy godmother had waved a magic wand.

A bed with a head and foot board crafted of thick tree limbs held a colorful patchwork quilt. Two down pillows topped the covering. Neat simple antique furniture filled the room, a small bureau, a tiny nightstand with a painted glass lamp, and a vanity dressing table similar to what he enjoyed in his room at Calin's. A neat bathroom included all the fixtures, including a claw-foot tub.

"What do you think?" asked Aaron. He turned and smiled at Blake.

"Quite a place. All of it." Blake eyes shone with interest.

"Do you see yourself living and working here?"

Blake's eyes widened. "Huh?"

"You heard me."

"I'd love nothing better. The condo I saw yesterday was none too shabby, but this takes the cake."

Aaron nodded. "Would you consider buying it?"

The question took Blake by surprise. "It's for sale? I didn't see a For Sale sign anywhere."

"The owners are selling it privately. They retired a few years ago. What they want is a buyer who will bring this place back to its former charm." Aaron touched Blake on the shoulder. "This will be a great place for working on designs for Mr. King. Remember our conversation yesterday?"

Blake looked around. He headed for the front door. Aaron didn't say anything but followed his student outside. Standing in the middle of the yard, Blake surveyed the land and surrounding woods, taking in every detail and placement of the buildings. From his estimation, everything seemed to be in reasonably good condition, work-ready, and easily accessible from the road.

There was plenty of space for parking if he decided to turn the shop back into a functioning one again. He lacked merchandise. The cabin was basically ready for moving in. Only groceries and necessities were needed.

"All these buildings have modern heat and air, if you didn't notice that before," said Aaron, stepping up beside Blake.

"I saw that. Electrical outlets everywhere, so I could set up machinery if I needed it."

"You're also not that far from town, Gatlinburg or Pigeon Forge. Or even Sevierville, for that matter." Aaron scratched his head, thinking. "Let me show you some of the surrounding property. There is some acreage here."

For several yards, the men walked through leaves, past trees, finally reaching the river. It was much bigger. Blake closed his eyes a few seconds, listening to the gurgling of the water. He inhaled a rich scent of leaves, dirt, honeysuckle, and a few other floral fragrances he couldn't readily identify.

"How much are they wanting for all this?" Blake turned to Aaron.

"How much you got? You've sold quite a bit of your farming inventions. Getting more orders every day."

"Enough to at least put a down payment on this property and make the monthly payments?" Blake met Aaron's gaze. "And still have money left to buy necessities and other things I might want?"

"If you're dead set on this deal, I'll get everything arranged with the family. They're selling it themselves and asked me to help because I'm an old friend of theirs. But that doesn't mean there aren't contracts to sign. All the fun legal things you have to do to make everything fair and square." Aaron smiled at Blake. "It's a great investment. You can't go wrong."

Blake nodded slowly. His mind whirled. Just yesterday, all he wanted was a simple condo where he could hang his hat and get on with his life. Now he was being presented with the hottest land deal in the Smoky Mountains. At least that's how he saw it.

"Yeah. Let's do it"

***

"I'm gonna miss you, son." Calin wiped the corner of his eye and sniffed. "Aw, look at me, carrying on like a silly girl." He squeezed Blake's arm, chuckling. "Never had kids. You're almost like my own. That's the way I feel, you know."

"Thanks for giving me a roof over my head and some money in my pocket. Don't know what I would have done without you." Blake stood next to his car, regarding the older man. He'd aged since they first met. As he viewed Calin, he acknowledged the slower gait, the stiffness in his movements. His hands had a slight tremor now.

"That's some danged fine property you got. I know exactly where it is. Anybody who knows anything about Gatlinburg knows where it is." Calin's lips pulled into a wide smile. "You'll do something mighty fine with that place. You're one smart fellow."

"Thanks, Calin. Good things have happened here. Never would have imagined it." Blake grinned. "You've taught me how to farm, deal with livestock, gave me an opportunity to launch a business. I owe you a lot."

"Glad to do it," said Calin.

Blake opened his car door and settled into the driver's seat. His belongings still fit in the duffle bag he'd brought from home four years ago. Trigger ran up, placing his paws on Blake's leg. "Hey, boy. I'm gonna miss you too." Blake scratched the dog behind the ears. "You and I have chased a lot of sheep, haven't we?"

Trigger barked and wagged his tail.

"Get yourself a dog when you settle in," said Calin.

"I might just do that. It's beautiful out there, but company would be nice."

Blake shut the car door, waved at Calin, and drove off. Deep in the heart of the Smokies, on Rapid Rivers Road, his new home sat waiting.

***

Blake parked his car under a shed near the cabin and turned off the engine. One thing he'd learned while Aaron showed him the property the first time was that a constant stream of cars rolled along Rapid Rivers Road during the day. This would be excellent for business. If he had signs made, surely people would stop and buy.

He got out of the car and headed toward the smaller building, the shop. Hard to believe the keys he held in his hand unlocked his home and his future. Blake squeezed them in his hand until it hurt. The pain reminded him that this wasn't a dream, a fantasy. It was as real as the water that rushed in the distance. As real as the cars that passed and the people in them. As real as the lock that accepted the key.

The inside of the shop sat waiting quietly for him. What would go on all the shelves, on the hooks, in the empty display baskets? His eyes wandered over all of it. He took in a deep breath, wondering for a moment if he hadn't bitten off more than he could chew. Maybe he shouldn't have gotten so eager and jumped at an opportunity without thinking it through in more detail.

The down payment on this place nearly wiped out half his savings, and the mortgage wasn't cheap, either. He didn't have Calin's safety net anymore, no matter how meager. Sales on his farm equipment gave him hope. He locked the shop and headed to the other building. This one held some options too. Just exactly what those options were lay dormant in his brain.

Too many directions he could take with this building. Did he want to keep one of the rooms for himself and rent out the other and the rest of the space? The Curious Peddler was one level, but he could make this space more.

"Knock, knock." A tiny voice called through the door.

Blake whirled around and found himself staring into Abby's face. Devon had come with her.

"Hey, guys!" Blake grinned, hugging Abby and shaking Devon's hand. "Missed me?"

"You bet," said Abby. "Professor Trolle has added some new volunteers, so that frees us up a little.

"Classes going okay?"

Both Abby and Devon nodded.

"I'm beginning to think I'll be in school forever," said Devon, laughing. "Going for masters and doctorates take time."

"Sucks to be you, right?" Blake lightly slapped Devon on the back.

"It's grueling, man."

Abby's eyes sparkled. "We really came to see if you needed any help. This whole place is gorgeous."

"What are you going to do with it?" asked Devon. He murmured, "Not to get too personal, but you got money for this?"

Blake exhaled and rubbed the back of his head. "Been asking myself just those same questions." He stared squarely at Abby and Devon. "I honestly don't have a clue what I need to do with this space."

"Do you want us to help you brainstorm, maybe come up with some ideas?"

"Are there any other students who may want to try out some of their ideas here, just like the shop in Gatlinburg?" Blake asked.

"I think you need to do some different things," said Abby. Her words came out with conviction. "Some similar gadgety items are okay, but customers may want things they can pick up easily without dropping down a chunk of change."

"Hate to say it, but I'm with her," said Devon, pointing to Abby.

"It leaves possibilities wide open." Blake shook his head, which ached a little.

Devon asked, "You gonna give us the grand tour?"

"Let's go," said Blake.

He showed them each building and the cabin. When they finished, Blake took them on a walk through the woods to the river. Abby slipped off her sandals and stepped in the water, squealing when her feet sank into unmerciful cold. Devon laughed. He bent over and splashed some water at her, laughing harder when she screamed and wiggled out of the way.

Blake couldn't help but notice how pretty she was, the sun lighting up her hair. Her skirt billowed out when she twirled on a large flat rock. For a moment he was envious. He wanted her. But she had her man. And to think her extended gazes and handshakes when they first met had meant something. How foolish could he have been?

Both he and Devon had lost. Her Mr. Right had scored himself the finest woman he could think of. Out of the blue, the vision came to him again, hit him full force. On the rock he saw her, a wispy ghostly form that seemed almost real. Red lips and pretty flowers.

"Hey," Blake said. He tapped Devon on the arm. "Have you seen that girl again?"

"What?" Devon asked, wrinkling his brow. "What are you talking about?"

"You know, the one we saw that night when we were at the bar?"

Devon stood with a questioning look on his face.

"The night I took you home," added Blake, emphasizing each word.

"Maybe another time or so?" Devon shook his head like he was clearing out cobwebs in his brain.

"How could you not remember seeing her again?"

"What's it to you?" Devon asked, his face clouding with irritation. "If I remember correctly, she bought me a drink."

"Yes, that she did." Blake turned his attention back on Abby.

"Aaand, maybe's she's bought me another one." Devon grinned at Blake.

"Good. Good for you. You need a drink every now and then." Blake couldn't resist the next question. "You ask her out, yet?"

"Are you kidding?" Devon's words hissed in Blake's ear. "These things have to be handled delicately, with finesse."

"Are you serious? She a girl, Devon, not some animal you're trying to lure into a trap. You just go up and ask."

"Are you that experienced?" Devon blurted out.

Blake turned around and stared his friend in the face. "Have you even talked to her, or do you just sit at the bar and make googly eyes at her?"

"Listen, dude, I'll handle this my way." Devon chuckled. "I got this. All in good time, my friend."

Blake shook his head. Devon's quick turn in attitude came at a good time. While his buddy seemed like he had all the time in the world, an inner time clock kept ticking for him. Tick. Tock. Tick. Tock. He only had this year to make everything work.

Later that afternoon, Aaron came by with food from the Cobbly Nob Mill Family Restaurant. They all gathered around the table in Blake's kitchen, eating and sipping wine. Everyone brainstormed, throwing out ideas to make Blake's future business, whatever it was, a success.

When they went home, Blake made a cup of coffee and sat on the front porch. Through openings in the trees, stars shimmered in the night sky. If he listened hard enough he heard the water. Crickets chirped. The occasional bird twittered. Spending time with Aaron, Abby, and Devon in his new surroundings had done him a world of good.

He thought about poor Calin all alone, probably watching TV in his living room. Tomorrow the older gentleman would have to manage the farm by himself. A sudden pang of sadness washed over him. Though he loved the surrounding beauty and held high hopes for the future, there lingered a sense of loneliness. Blake decided he would have to take Calin's advice and get a dog.

Chapter Six

He'd stalled. No way around it. No two twos about it. His brain had shut down for some reason. Had all the education, design work, calculations, and marketing done him in? Blake surely felt like it. Sipping coffee, he sat on a stool behind an empty checkout counter. As he looked through a dusty window, cars rolled by. Always coming, never stopping.

Blake's mood turned gloomier with each passing car. Without a steady income, his funds trickled away each day, putting him at risk of going bankrupt before starting anything. Several weeks in this new place, and no great ideas to kickstart something great.

He'd spent hours on the internet, walking the Gatlinburg strip, and even spent time in Pigeon Forge checking out the shops. Blake wanted to kick himself in the pants for stopping work at Calin's. He could have commuted back and forth for a while. People did it every day.

But purchasing this property rescued him from a lifestyle he never wanted in the first place. He considered himself a city slicker, a business person who made deals in offices and hobnobbed with contacts at parties. If he had to spend another day slopping pigs, chasing sheep, or working in a garden, he'd go crazy.

Sales on his inventions had taken an unexplained nosedive. Maybe he should ask Calin if he could join him at the farmer's market. Do another sales pitch. Show some videos. Liven his life back up again. Working at The Curious Peddler—for free—wasn't the answer, either. He couldn't work there and here at the same time.

He needed to remove his displays from The Curious Peddler and set up shop in the larger building where there was ample space. Aaron kindly let him keep his display up and running, but who was he kidding? Abby had lost interest in pushing his work. Devon always avoided it. Pure luck sold his machines in that store. They drastically differed from the cutesy items Devon and Abby created.

Emptiness in the small shop he sat in now stared back at him, an expanse growing larger the longer he muddled through the confusion clouding his mind. What did he want on the shelves? Disgusted, he sipped from his mug, admitting that the cutesy items in Aaron's business made the sales. People wanted things they could afford and take home without a price tag breaking the bank. Did he want the same items as before when the original owners ran the shop? Was it time for a change? Maybe he needed to ask Calin for his old job back.

"Maybe you need to stop dreaming and get to work."

Blake's eyes flew open. When he turned around, he saw Aaron leaning against the door frame.

"Hey. How's it going?"

"Just passing through. But it would be much better for you if you got going. On something." Aaron walked toward the shelves. "Why haven't you talked to Les?"

"Who?"

"Lesander King. That letter you read in my office . . . oh, I don't know . . . eons ago."

Blake grimaced. "I want to be set up first, have a business name, some equipment."

"At the rate you're going, this place will be in foreclosure." Aaron shot his former student a warning glance. "I emailed you all the information. If you're stuck, maybe Les can get you unstuck. By the way, I need your space at The Curious Peddler. Devon has some new items to put out, and we don't have any other room."

"I'll get everything today." Blake studied Aaron's face.

"Do it today after you meet with Les." Aaron turned and left.

His teacher hadn't seemed angry, but he could tell by the tightness in Aaron's jaw that he meant business. So Devon had some new projects to sell. This news sent Blake into panic mode plus. The world was passing him by, and it scared him.

He pulled out his cell phone. Neither Jared nor Shorty had called. Still. In four years. He thought the more time passed, the desire to keep in touch with family would dwindle. Now he wanted to call them more than ever, but his inner stubbornness dug in its heels. It seemed his family had truly written him off. Would they help if he asked?

Blake locked up the shop and headed back to his cabin. This time, he intended to follow through on Aaron's suggestion. Sitting at a quaint little desk purchased from a local antique mall, he opened his laptop and scrolled, locating Aaron's email. It was now or never. If he didn't do this, he might as well go curl up in a corner and cry. Blake tapped at the numbers and waited.

"King Enterprises." A perky female voice spoke into his ear.

Blake sat up straighter, startled. The voice touched him in a way he couldn't readily explain.

"King Enterprises. Can I help you?"

"Yes. I'm calling because Aaron Trolle suggested I talk to Mr. King," said Blake. His mind whirled. What would he say?"

"May I ask what this is regarding?"

She sounded pretty, whomever she was.

"I understand he's looking for designers. I know engineering and have some products I've developed and sold."

"Wonderful. Let me check our calendar." There was a pause. "We have an opening next Tuesday at three o'clock."

The information disappointed Blake. Today was Monday.

"Is there anything sooner? I'm looking forward to meeting with him."

"I'm so sorry, but he's booked solid. Do you have a number? I can put you on a cancellation list."

"Sure." Blake gave her his cell phone number. "I really appreciate it. Please call me if I can see him sooner."

"I'd be delighted to do that. I have you down for next Tuesday. We appreciate your call."

And that was it. Nothing to do but wait. Blake scolded himself. Why had he not jumped on it when Aaron gave him the information? He could have already scored a meeting and been working on the next best thing on the planet.

In the meantime, he had no other choice but to pack up his goods from Aaron's shop and put them in his own. Somewhere. Blake let out a groan and headed to his car. Tuesday couldn't come soon enough.

***

Devon's eyes lit up when Blake walked onto the showroom floor. "Hey, buddy. Hate to do this to you, but I got some new pieces to sell."

"I get it. Totally cool." Blake glanced at Abby, whose mouth turned down in sympathetic sadness.

"I bet you can sell these where you are now," said Devon, pointing to Blake's farm equipment. "Oh, I forgot. You're really not open, yet, are you? That's too bad."

Abby shot Devon a buzzard-eye look and turned to Blake. "Is there anything else we can do to help? I know what it feels like to be stuck."

"Got something in the works." Blake showed the same intent look to Devon.

"Nice. What is it?" Devon asked, eyes narrowing.

"Don't want to say right now. Might jinx everything." Blake winked at Abby.

"Let us know if you need anything." Abby punched Devon in the arm. He scowled at her.

"Hey, Blake, I've got the truck out back. I'll help you load up." Aaron's voice rang out from the back of the shop. "Devon, when we clear out, it's all yours."

"Got it, Professor Trolle." Devon flashed Blake a toothy smile.

One by one, Blake loaded up his equipment in the shop truck.

"I'll loan you the laptop so you can show the videos, but I'll need it back soon." Aaron fastened his seat belt."

"I might can find a good refurb somewhere," said Blake. He closed the passenger door and strapped himself in.

"You might check with the university computer department. They might have one to sell at a cheap price, or just give you one. Never know unless you check it out."

"Good idea."

The men retraced the roads back to Blake's place. When they arrived, Aaron asked, "Any idea where you want to put these?" He pointed to the rear of the truck.

"Let's put them in the big building. That would be a good place." Blake nodded and licked his lower lip. It was as good a place as any. He could advertise them. A few changes to some websites and links, and he'd be up and rolling again. With any luck, it would be true.

"Did you make a phone call like I asked you?"

"All set for next Tuesday at three."

Aaron frowned. "That far out?" He shook his head. "I guess people are really jumping at a chance to be part of his team. I hope he doesn't fill his positions before you get a chance to talk to him."

"I got on their cancellation list." Blake hoped this last statement would make him feel somewhat better, but it didn't. Cancellations seemed iffy to him. That's what he felt in his gut.

"Let's get these inside and set up." Aaron got out of the truck.

An hour later, Blake found himself alone again. He headed back to his buildings, this time taking a vacuum cleaner and cleaning supplies. At least he would feel like he was doing something productive. Scrolling through the internet and trying to find merchandise and suppliers for his store had also been a bust.

Later that night, he sat on his front porch again, coffee in hand, rocking, and staring at the stars. He needed a legitimate business name, fast. For several minutes, Blake racked his brain, running some potential names through his head. He didn't know where it came from or why it landed on the porch railing. All he knew was the rush of wings as it flew past sent him bounding from his rocker.

His coffee cup crashed on the wooden planks, breaking in three big pieces. Blake swore and looked at what made the disturbance. A large owl had flown across the porch, nearly crashing into him. Why would an owl do such a thing? Had his porch lights attracted or confused it in any way?

The large bird studied Blake with a penetrating stare, let out a couple of mournful hoots, and flew away into the night. He let out a loud sigh of relief and spent the next several minutes cleaning up coffee. The bad news, his favorite mug had been destroyed. The good news, he now had a name for his business.

Blake sat down at his desk. When he updated links and the location for purchasing his farm equipment, he input the new business name: Hoot Owl Hollow.

***

Tuesday. The big day had arrived, and Blake sat with sweaty palms waiting to meet with Lesander King. The youthful attractive voice he'd heard on the phone didn't match the matronly lady who sat at the reception desk today. Was she Lesander's wife or hired help? He remembered times when Eileen had spent hours answering phones, taking orders, and directing people where they needed to go.

Located on one of the state highways on the far side of Gatlinburg, Lesander King's office appeared modest for someone who appeared to have a reputation for big business. Neat and attractive, the waiting room had two other people besides Blake. He'd been disappointed in seeing anyone. More people to snag a position before he could get one for himself.

When the second person had gone back, Blake pulled out his cell phone and glanced at the time. The late afternoon was becoming much later. Did all of the appointments run over like this? He looked up at the sound of someone rustling near him. It was the last man who had just met with the owner.

The man's face seemed a little constricted, like the meeting hadn't gone so well. From what Blake remembered, the first person's face didn't look like he'd been to a tea party, either. He couldn't resist. "Hey," he called out, signaling the man's attention. "How did it go?"

"He's tough. Looking for about five people, and he said he's been interviewing for a while."

"Oh," answered Blake. "Sounds like stiff competition."

The young man nodded and walked out the front office door. Blake sank down in his chair, disheartened. How different was he from the others? In his mind, designers came a dime a dozen. They all held degrees, had different levels of experience. How vast were the differences?

Lesander King almost reminded him of his father. Jared's quirks and peculiarities ran hard and fast with the quirkiest, most peculiar one out there. More than anything he wanted to know the real reason for the split between King and his dad. But that was another question for another time and day.

"Mr. McCallahan, Mr. King will see you now." The matronly lady looked in Blake's direction. "His office is at the end of the hallway. You can't miss it."

Blake got up, ignoring the clenching in his gut. It was make or break. He'd either succeed or completely flop. If he succeeded, his dreams for a prosperous business lay in the palm of his hand. If he flopped, he was on his own, flying solo, and no family to back him up. Worse, this was like trying to win approval from his father all over again. His stomach hurt.

He knocked on the door with the nameplate Lesander King engraved on it.

"Come in." Mr. King's voice rang out.

From the look of the refined gentleman sitting behind the desk, Blake couldn't help but detect a slight fatigue in the man's eyes. This could be good or bad. Good in the possibility that he might just wave Blake and his accomplishments on to one of the positions. Bad for the same reason. Anything said or not presented just right could highly irritate him.

"Have a seat, young man." Mr. King pointed to a vacant chair in front of the desk.

Blake sat down, suddenly at a loss on what to do with his hands, other than hold them primly in his lap. He prayed his heart didn't explode from anxiety.

"I understand you have some engineering and design experience?" Mr. King asked. He got up from behind his desk and sat down in the other vacant chair across from Blake.

"Yes, sir."

"Do you have a copy of your resumé?"

Blake's eyes widened. Why he didn't create one escaped his faculties at the moment. Had he grown complacent? For the first time, he admitted life once handed him everything.

"You did bring one, didn't you?" Mr. King's eyes glinted with a steely coldness that sent Blakes's nerves on edge.

"No, Mr. King, I didn't."

The businessman drummed his fingers on the arm of his chair. "And why would you even bother to come here without one? I'm a busy man, Mr. McCallahan, and I don't have time for game-playing. I surely don't like people wasting my time, either. If you don't have anything better, then maybe we need to end this interview right here and now."

"Sir," said Blake, "I don't think a resumé would really do justice to what I've accomplished." His nerve had kicked in, and a new spark of energy flooded through him. "If you have a computer, I can answer all your questions."

Mr. King's face lightened. "Come over here." He ushered Blake to another smaller table in the office. On it sat a laptop. "Show me what you got."

"I'd be more than happy to, Mr. King. I'm hoping that my work and experience will make me worthy of one of your positions."

"I'm hoping so, too, Mr. McCallahan, because it's getting later in the day, and my patience is wearing thin."

"Yes, sir." Blake's heart sank. Not what he wanted at all. He felt like he'd already started off the meeting at rock bottom. Nowhere to go but up.

With a few taps on the keypad, Blake showed Mr. King each webpage listing his projects. Hoot Owl Hollow had a brand new domain and web site, complete with information and pricing. For several minutes, they watched the videos Blake had created.

"This is impressive," said Mr. King, smiling. "You sell these?"

"I've sold several units. I purchased some new property, so I have my shop set up there. I had everything at The Curious Peddler."

The older gentlemen stared at Blake. "The one owned by Aaron Trolle? He's a professor at the university. Are you a student of his?"

"Was," said Blake. "I finished everything with him not long ago."

"You have a bachelors or a masters?"

"Neither." Blake turned his eyes back to the laptop.

"How's that?" Lesander King's eyes narrowed. His fingers tapped on the table.

Blake knew he had some explaining to do. He updated the gentleman on the arrangement he had with Aaron and talked briefly about his family work history.

"If you had a pretty good deal at home, why on earth would you ever want out of it? Especially if it made some good money?" Mr. King's eyes narrowed.

"There's a time when you want to break away from the family. Do your own thing, make your own way. Until you're truly the one at the helm calling the shots, you really never are." Blake eyed the man sitting next to him, hoping he wouldn't ask any more questions about his past.

Lesander King stroked his chin for a few seconds. "I gotta hand it to you. That's pretty much on the money." He stood up. "Come here. I want to show you something."

Blake followed the man to a door leading into another room. From a small drawer, one of many in a long built-in row of shelving, Mr. King pulled out a long shiny wooden box. He walked to a table in the middle of the room and sat down, motioning for Blake to do the same.

"I want you to see these," said Mr. King. He flipped on a brass lamp sitting on the table and pulled it toward him. "What I have in here is something you'll not find anywhere." He released the tiny latch and lifted the lid. A big smile lit up his face. "And there you have it. Aren't they beautiful?"

"They are . . . yeah . . . interesting." Blake sat perplexed, nodding and staring into a neat row of nine tiny compartments. In each compartment lay a small shiny gold pig.

"You want to hold one?" Lesander King lifted one little pig out of its resting place.

Blake took it gently between his thumb and forefinger, gazing at it with interest. The pig was no more than three inches high, and it had arms and legs that dangled down, swinging lightly when he moved the piece. The figurines were meant to stand upright as if they had human qualities. As they were now, they would not stay in place once posed.

"What do you do with them?" He looked at Mr. King and returned the pig.

"Best question I've had all day. You know why?"

Blake shook his head.

"Because you're the first person who's seen them." Mr. King grinned. "Out of all the people I've interviewed—and I've interviewed some good ones—I've not found one I thought would be very helpful." He leaned close to Blake. "You see, I have no idea what to do with these. The answer eludes me, for some reason."

"Where did you get them?"

"I've had them for a while. They were given as a gift from one of my sponsors, and all they do is take up residence in that drawer over there." Mr. King pointed to the drawer from where he removed the box. "I'm dying to do something with them. They're kind of cute, if you know what I mean."

"Why show them to me?" Blake asked.

"Because I suspect you're just the person who can create something of interest with these tiny, adorable, confounding piglets."

"Fantastic." Blake sank back in his chair, beaming with joy. But somewhere inside, a twinge of fear set in.

Mr. King's statements sounded like the sweetest blessing. This is what he'd been looking for, the reason he left home. The reason he signed on with Aaron and The Curious Peddler. The reason he endured farm living for so long. He'd be a fool to say no. But he had not banked on a project such as this.

What started out as a doubtful interview had blossomed into a precious gift, even if it had a little twist. The important factor, the project had been handed to him only. He'd find something creative to do with these pigs or die trying. He had spent his time building useful tools commanding handsome prices. Abby and Devon had focused on the artsy tasks. Now it was his turn to try his hand at it.

"Are you up for the task, young man?" asked Mr. King. "It will put you in the running for a position on my team." He tapped on the table. "Trust me, you want a place on my team. I sell all kinds of unique gifts and oddities that fetch a pretty nice price. Gifts for the elite. You know, the gift you buy someone who has everything?"

"I'll take these little trinkets and see what I can come up with."

"Do whatever you need to do. Use your best judgment." Lesander King laid the pig inside its compartment and closed the lid. "Have fun." He smiled.

"I love challenges, sir." Blake picked up the box.

"I'll favorite your business website. Call me in four months. Sound good?"

"Sounds good to me."

Mr. King escorted Blake to the reception desk and waved goodbye.

The matronly lady smiled. "Looks like you won him over. I've never seen anyone walk out of here with one of his belongings. Good job."

"Wish me luck. I'm going to need it." Blake smiled back at the lady and headed out the door.

Blake placed the box on the passenger's side and started the engine. His mind whirled. What would he fashion out of the box of pigs? He backed out of the parking lot. Time to celebrate—or cry. He sped down the road toward the Gatlinburg strip. Once he found a spot in a public parking lot, he hid the precious box in his trunk, and headed to the bar he and Devon had frequented.

He ordered a seafood platter and some beer. This overall was a celebration. He'd think of something creative to please Lesander King. But despite the happiness in securing a chance to work with Mr. King, something else overshadowed his success. Another mystery as murky as the golden pigs. The golden box. Each day the homestretch lessened, leading into a stark reality he didn't necessarily like. He had to be a married man before the end of this year.

When he put the two in perspective and compared them, dealing with the pigs would be much easier. Did Abby have any girlfriends he could date? He could ask Aaron if he knew of any young students. Maybe Calin knew of someone. Panic hit him full force. Whatever was in that gold box, he didn't want to lose it. Jared hadn't shared much, but he wouldn't have given it to Blake for fun and games.

Starting tomorrow, he would actively start working on dating. Engineering was a male-dominated profession. He had enough money to take at least one class. Then he'd check out the women. He could join a fraternity. No, he was too old for that now.

"Here's your order." A cute waitress came up to his table, placing a steaming plate in front of him. "Anything else I can get you?"

"Another beer, please."

"Coming right up."

Blake picked up his fork and plunged it into his food. He stared out the window, watching people pass by. His heart nearly stopped. Blonde hair, thin figure, flower. He rubbed his eyes, blinked, and looked again. Was that her? The girl he'd seen with Devon?

He looked harder but couldn't tell. A small crowd of people blocked his view. Blake craned his neck, trying to get another look. It was too late. The woman disappeared when everyone cleared. He mentally added another item on his project list: go out with Devon more. If the beautiful one liked Devon, she surely had a friend who might like him.

Unfortunately, there was only one catch. He wanted the beauty for himself.

Chapter Seven

Blake sat in the old shop building at Hoot Owl Hollow, staring at an open box of sparkling little pigs. He'd first carried the box with him into the large building, standing in every room and location to see if his muse would pop out and show off a bit. He thought a certain special room or location might do the trick. The Feng Shui thing people talked about. Nothing.

He stared at the box, trying to send himself into some sort of meditative trance. Maybe an idea would come to him. What did he think of when he saw piglets like this? Never mind the fact he'd never seen anything like them before, until Lesander King whipped out his trusty box from a line of drawers.

"Whatever it is, it must be the most fascinating thing in the whole wide world." Blake saw Aaron walking toward him. "Mind if I have a look?"

"Be my guest." Blake leaned away, allowing Aaron a view of the box.

The professor furrowed his brows. "Where on earth did you get these?"

"Lesander King gave them to me." Blake smiled his biggest.

"No!" Aaron let out a quick laugh and stepped back. "Why?"

"If I can figure out what to do with them, I get a spot on his team. And I'm the only one he's given anything to. He told me so." Blake nodded.

Aaron's eyes narrowed. "Any ideas?"

"Not a clue."

"Hmm. Keep thinking, and I'll think too. Somewhere we'll meet in the middle." Aaron tapped on the counter top with his knuckles. "I want you to be successful at this."

"Me too." Blake blurted out something next that took him by surprise. "How do you win the love of your life before this year is over?"

"Say what?" Aaron asked. "What does that have to do with your project?"

"That's a legitimate question."

"So was mine."

Blake exhaled in a huff. "Remember what I told you about the deal I made with my father? Being married by the end of five years, or else?"

Aaron's eyes narrowed. "Or else what? You didn't go into that much detail before."

"Beats me. My dad wouldn't say."

"I still say your dad's weird."

"There's something at stake," said Blake. "And I don't know what it is, but my dad's a lot like Lesander King. He means everything he says."

Aaron's gaze penetrated Blake. "I can help you with the pigs. When it comes to love and marriage, that's where I drop off." He shook his head. "You'll have to find your own way on that one, my friend." He turned and left the shop.

Blake listened to Aaron's car roar off down the road. He stepped out from behind the counter and walked around the shop. He needed an idea. Fast. His eye caught something glistening on the bottom of one of the shelves. He blinked a few times to see if it was real. He'd checked out everything in every nook and cranny inside both buildings and even his cabin.

How could he have missed this? He squatted in front of the shelf. It looked like a wine bottle had been forgotten. Curious, he reached out and pulled it toward him. His eyes widened with surprise. The bottle wasn't an ordinary one you'd find in a liquor store, unless they sold gifts or commemorative items too.

He picked it up carefully and peered into the glass. Inside stood a tiny ballerina dancer encased in a glass dome. Her hands were positioned in the style of a ballet dancer, and her tiny legs ended en pointe. She wore a simple white dress with golden stars on it. Blake turned the bottle sideways.

On the bottom, he viewed what looked like the workings of a music box. He gently turned the key, praying he wouldn't break anything. A tiny tinkling sound trickled out. Blake positioned the bottle on a higher shelf and watched in amazement as the lady whirled around a spindle running up the length of her body.

The tiny pointed shoes clicked against the base of the dome as the figure lifted up, touched down, and whirled around again in the opposite direction. Blake's pulse raced as he watched the miniature lady for several minutes.

Why couldn't he do something similar with the golden pigs? He picked up the bottle, the box of pigs, and walked back to his cabin. Seated at his desk, he pulled out a sketch book where he made some rudimentary drawings and calculations. After he wrote down the last note, he researched more on the internet.

If the previous owners made a decent living in the shop space he owned now, why not replicate what they did, with some personal modifications? There was no need to overthink this whole operation, and not everything changed all of the time. He got in his car and headed to Gatlinburg strip.

Necessity was the mother of invention, and he would not wait any longer. Moving through crowds of tourists, Blake headed to the sign maker's shop he saw the day Aaron returned the wallet.

"What can I do for you?" The artisan stopped his burning tool and glanced up at Blake.

"Can you make me some signs for a business?"

"I can make anything you want. Just tell me what it is." The young man smiled.

Blake spent the next few minutes describing dimensions and outlining what he wanted on each.

"Tell you what. I'll work on them now. If you can hang around the strip for a while, you'll have everything in a couple of hours."

"I'll be back before you close. Thanks, buddy. Appreciate you." Blake smiled and left the shop. He headed toward The Curious Peddler. Time to ask Abby if she had any nice female friends.

Three days later, Blake found himself sitting with a nice attractive lady at The Cobbly Nob Mill Family Restaurant. Things were starting to look much better.

***

Blake drove the second pole into the ground and wiped away the sweat dripping down his forehead and the sides of his face. Already he felt better, even if he was tired. Any step toward making his business into a reality made him feel better. The fact that he'd gone on a date brightened his spirits too. He wanted to ask the lady out again.

While he daydreamed about another date, he added hooks and chains to the poles and hung up the two custom-made signs purchased in Gatlinburg. The top one said "Hoot Owl Hollow—Gifts & Curiosities." The one under it said "Artisans Wanted." Blake included his business cell number. He already updated his web site with information on how crafters could contact him.

Inside his shop, shelves gleamed, clean and polished. Displays stood ready for new merchandise. The checkout counter looked spic and span with sparkling glass showing some new antique items. Blake had contacted Calin and the two attended an auction. Calin gladly gifted him several jars of pickled eggs and beets, butter pickles, relish, and hot sauces he'd made and canned.

"I think this will go real nice in your shop, son." The older man had dropped off the goods personally so he could see Blake's new home. "You'll have a top-notch setup once you get it all going."

Blake's business cell rang. "Hoot Owl Hollow. May I help you? Yes . . . I'd be very interested in seeing your skin care line. I think soaps and body cream would be wonderful. Yes, I have space. I'll be open until 6 p.m."

He smiled. He'd have the shelves filled in no time. Just as he walked back inside his shop, Aaron showed up.

"I have something for you." He smiled and laid a tin pipe on the counter.

"What is that?" Blake's eyes narrowed.

"A tin whistle. Or maybe you've heard the term penny whistle."

Blake picked up the instrument. "Does it work?"

"It's cleaned and sanitized. Go ahead. Give it a few toots."

Blake put the tip to his mouth and blew. A sharp whistle came out the other end. He moved his fingers on and off the holes, creating a series of different sounding notes and pitches. "And what exactly am I supposed to do with it? Did you have others you want me to sell?" He grinned.

"Nope," said Aaron, laughing. "I've given you a penny whistle. Figure the rest out." He turned out of the building, disappearing as fast as he'd come.

"That man gets more cryptic every time I see him," Blake muttered to himself.

A couple of hours later, the lady who called Blake earlier stopped by the shop. He approved her merchandise, made his selection, and paid her. Now he had a shelf with soaps, lotions, lip balms, and body cream, all hand-crafted and packaged in tidy jars and attractive labeling. He picked out some of her perfume oils too. Another lady came by, showing her line of crocheted scarves, hats, and small blanket throws.

"I like the way they feel, and the colors are nice," said Blake.

The lady smiled. "I make the yarn myself. I also have some felted change purses, if you'd like some of them. Nice little gifts people can pick up. I try to keep my prices as affordable as possible."

"Let's do it. I'll buy some items from you." Blake pulled out his check book and paid the woman. She stayed around, helping him arrange everything on some shelves and displays.

Customers pulled off the road and came inside, curious.

"Welcome," said Blake, smiling. "I'm new. I'll be adding lots more merchandise, but this is what I have today."

To his relief, people made purchases. One nice lady selected a vintage necklace from inside the glass checkout counter.

"It will look really nice on you," said Blake. "Would you like to wear it out?"

"I'd love to." The lady allowed Blake to fasten it around her neck.

While people shopped, a gentleman called and asked if he could come by the next day to show some of his pieces he'd crafted with wood-turning skills, vases, trinket boxes, and figurines. Blake penciled him in on his calendar and eyed an empty shelf that would display the man's collection quite nicely.

He ran a tally on his sales. Not bad for an impromptu opening. All he needed was a neon "Open" sign to hang inside the window. At six o'clock, another person stepped into the shop.

"Hey Abby." Blake hugged his friend.

Abby looked around the store. "You're filling this place up. Looks great."

"Made some sales with what I've got so far." Somehow he detected an uncomfortable look on Abby's face. He'd sensed it the moment she walked through the door, and he knew she wasn't coming to visit for the heck of it. "Did your friend say anything about our date? I'm thinking about asking her out again."

"About that." Abby bit her lower lip. She walked over to one of the scarves and ran her fingers over the surface.

"What 'about that?'" asked Blake. He didn't like the tone in her voice.

"She said you were really sweet, but there just wasn't any interest on her part."

"Oh." Blake's heart sank. He walked over to the door and placed a temporary "Closed" sign along with the store hours on the outside. "Was it something I said, or did I do something wrong?"

"I think she just felt like you were uncomfortable with her, or that you seemed awkward."

"Really?" Blake frowned a moment. "Odd. Because we laughed and seemed to have a good time."

"Don't know." Abby shook her head in thought. "I think you saw it one way, and she saw it another. I think we need to try for someone new."

Blake forced a smile and a more animated expression. "I'm game. The feeling has to be mutual, you know?"

"Aw, Blake. You're a sweetheart of a guy. She was only one girl. And I'll admit, she has her quirks. A good friend, but still."

"No need to apologize. She was still really nice."

"I'll go over my list of friends and their friends." Abby rubbed Blake's arm. "There's someone out there just for you. You're a special guy."

"Thanks, Abby."

She waved and opened the door, leaving him alone, stewing in pure disappointment. Blake sighed. He had hoped for success, but few people landed their mate on the first try. Time was running out for him. He should have worked on this from day one.

Worse, he fumed that his dad would put him in such a precarious position. Jared would never marry Eileen. He knew that now. They'd been together too long with nothing heading down the aisle. If he had the gold box in his immediate possession instead of locked away in a safe deposit box at the bank, he'd smash it to smithereens and take a peek inside.

What was the worst that could happen? He would lose favor with his dad? He'd forfeit a big prize? Blake turned off the lights to the shop and headed back to the cabin. After dinner, he headed to the local hardware store. Girl or no girl, he still had tiny golden pigs he had to deal with.

***

Held firmly in a padded vice, one of the pigs had been positioned upside down. Blake took a deep breath. He couldn't mess up. One wrong drill hole, and the whole figure would be useless. All he needed was a hole in the bottom.

He selected one of the rooms in the large building as his personal work space. Once he fixed the pig the way he wanted it, he'd take everything to the shop where he could work more on it when he didn't have customers.

Blake picked up a tiny nail and hammer. Positioning the nail exactly where he wanted the hole, he tapped hard enough to put an indention in the metal. Good start. His power drill lay charged and ready. Carefully, he placed the drill tip in the indention and turned on the tool.

The metal was soft enough to take the bit and allow a small hole in the bottom of the pig. Blake took a cotton cloth and swiped off the metal shavings. He unscrewed the vice and removed the pig. The next part was equally unnerving. He had decided he wanted the arms of the figurine bent, one arm in front and the other in back. The legs stayed the same.

He picked up two pairs of padded pliers so he wouldn't mark up the metal. Holding an arm firmly midway, he grasped the other end with the other pliers and bent the metal with slow even pressure. The only thing he didn't like was the crinkle at the bend.

Blake picked up a small file and rounded out the arms, shaving down the pointy areas. Didn't look too bad. These were really prototypes for the real thing, if this project worked. He looked at the clock on the wall. Time to open the shop.

The man with the wooden boxes came as promised. Soon another shelf held attractive merchandise. While customers browsed, Blake worked on his pig, studying how he would insert and attach the spindle so the figurine would twirl on a base. Blake made a few more detailed notes and drawings in the notebook he'd brought with him.

He wrote an email to Aaron with a list of what he needed to create a mechanized base that worked like most musical jewelry boxes, with a crank mechanism and the notched drum and prongs that created the music when the drum rotated. Just as he was about to press the send button, he stopped.

His gaze fell on the penny whistle carelessly tossed aside on one end of the counter. Blake had almost forgotten about it. What was Aaron thinking? He pulled out his phone to call but put it back in his pocket. His teacher had told him to "figure it out." This had to be his project, not Aaron's.

Throughout the day, several customers bought items and left. He also received a call from a person interested in the AutoTrough. When he had a spare moment, Blake picked up the whistle and blew. The idea hit him swift and hard. He wouldn't create a piece like the dancer in the wine bottle. That was rather cliché. He'd make his pig more interactive, unique.

When 6 p.m. rolled around, Blake closed up shop and drove to The Curious Peddler.

***

Abby nodded as Blake talked. They left Devon to run the front while they chatted in the work room.

"I have an idea, and you are the only one I trust, besides Aaron," said Blake.

"What is it?" Abby asked.

Blake brought her up to speed on the pig and what he wanted to do. "This is going to work much differently than I had originally planned."

"You're talking about something more than simple mechanics." Abby shook her head. "This involves more, and I haven't studied it myself. There is a program at the university where you can learn it."

"I don't have that kind of time." He gazed up at the ceiling. "I just don't seem to have much time for anything right now. Everything is running out on me."

"You procrastinate a lot?"

"Just on one thing." He smiled at the attractive woman beside him.

"I got another friend who said she'd go out with you."

"I'm on it. Give me the details, and I'll call her."

"I'll give you that and a special contact person at the university who can help with your project." She scribbled a few lines on a piece of paper and handed it to Blake. "Sorry, but your project is over my head." Abby smiled.

"You're a real pal, Abby." A bold streak hit him. "Honestly, if you didn't have that fiancé of yours, I would have asked you out long ago."

"You're sweet, Blake. I do have a favor to ask, though."

***

Bright and early, Blake stepped out of his cabin and into his car. Today, he was going to school. Not for class, but to follow up on Abby's contact. The young man, a teaching assistant named Eric, had been more than glad to meet up and talk about the pig project. And tonight Blake was in store for another date.

But one thing floored his mind the most. Abby's favor. She wanted to have her wedding at Hoot Owl Hollow. As he sped down the interstate, he wondered at the irony of it all. He needed a wife. She wanted his home for a wedding location. If he got married—and he would do it—his property would have already been christened in the wedding way. He chuckled to himself. With any luck his date would end up with him winning Miss Right.

Blake took the exit ramp leading to the university. Traffic had set in for rush hour, and the constant stopping and starting irritated him. He thanked his lucky stars he'd never had to deal much with traffic, but got up, got dressed, and walked a few yards to the office he and his father shared.

Eric had kindly emailed a parking pass and instructions on where to park, which would save time. Students already walked the sidewalks, backpacks in tow. Youthful, strong, determined. The future of mankind in the making right before his eyes. At once he felt his age, and the infernal time clock ticked on, never stopping.

Student life had to be an experience like no other. A breath of fresh air with the world at your fingertips, waiting just for you. Freedom from family, on your own, making many of your own decisions, meeting all kinds of new people.

Blake reminded himself that he'd experienced things most people wanted. The only reason these students paid ungodly fortunes to hike the walkways and stairs to class was to have what he once had. He'd been blessed in many ways. Why did he have a hard time embracing that fact at times?

He wound through the streets of campus and found his way to the designated lot. One space left for him, and he barely got it before another car pulled in. Inside the College of Engineering, he took in the view of polished floors, rows of doors, and students passing through. His classroom in Aaron's kitchen for the last four years was nothing like what these students had to endure.

Blake peeped inside a large lecture hall. A pang of anxiety blasted through him. Too many people, and way too formal for his taste. He walked the floors to the assistant's office.

"Hi." A man looked up from his desk and stacked a few papers in place. "You made it through all the traffic, I see." He pointed to a vacant chair.

"It's hard when you don't have to do it every day." Blake smiled and sat down.

"I bet. Lucky you." Eric smiled. "What you got? Abby didn't tell me too much."

"It's an unusual project, not like the big ones you deal with here. And it's not like the big ones I've created, either."

"When it comes to making money, it all counts. I'd love to hear what you're working on." Eric sat back in his chair, arms resting behind his head.

Eric seemed like an unassuming guy. Relaxed with soft eyes and an easy demeanor. Unlike Devon, who harbored a bit of arrogance and way too much competition and jealousy. If this was the guy with the answers, Blake knew he'd like working with him.

"It goes like this . . ." Blake explained his situation with the golden pigs, minus where he got them. The last thing he wanted was several more engineers running to Lesander King.

Eric nodded slowly as Blake talked, narrowing his eyes at times in concentration. When Blake finished, he said, "Let me show you something. You got some time?"

"I have to be back at my shop at least by ten o'clock."

"Won't take long, but it may be just the answer you're looking for."

The two men took an elevator down to the bottom floor of the engineering building. Eric escorted Blake inside a large room.

"This is one of our labs. We have several, you know." Eric delivered a pointed look at Blake.

"From the size of this place, it doesn't surprise me." Blake smiled in interest.

"What you're needing involves sound patterns. When you capture the frequencies and they're mimicked, you can use them to instigate motion or whatever you want to happen."

Eric led Blake to a counter. On it stood a machine that looked like a recording device capable of not only accepting sound but printing out the sound waves on paper. "I've been working on something similar to what you're needing. Did you happen to bring your sound source with you, or did you have something else in mind?"

Blake's eyes widened. "Sorry, but I didn't know how much detail we were going into today, so no."

"Let me see. I might have something in here that might work, just to show you how your project might go." Eric walked to a cabinet and pulled out a plastic flutophone. "We'll try this."

The assistant flipped a few buttons, re-calibrated the machine, and started it. He blew several notes into the flutophone, and the waves printed out, showing the highs, lows, and sustaining sounds. "Now we'll do this," said Eric.

He pulled out what looked like a flash drive and inserted it into another device holding a small wheel. Eric turned on the tiny machine and blew into the flutophone once again, switching up the notes. To Blake's amazement and delight, the wheel turned. The faster Eric blew, the faster the wheel moved.

"Is that kind of what you're looking for?" Eric looked up at Blake, his eyes shining.

"I do believe that's exactly what I'm looking for."

"Tell you what, let's get together again. Bring me everything you're using for your project, and I'll have a look at it. We'll go from there."

"When?" asked Blake. "I don't know about your schedule, but for me, the quicker the better."

"How about this Thursday. We'll get some recordings, and I'll give you the flash drive with the sounds. You can take it from there."

"I owe you a lot. Thanks for the time." Blake shook Eric's hand.

"No problem, buddy. I should thank you for letting me and Abby use your place for our wedding."

Chapter Eight

All the way back to Rapid Rivers Road, Blake couldn't get Eric's last words out of his head. Eric and Abby. She had been right. Her fiancé had the knowledge to help with his project, but why she hadn't told him who Eric was beforehand mystified him.

Blake pulled his car under the shed and opened his shop. Thursday he hoped much of his problems would be solved with his current project. The pig was ready, and now all he needed was the sound. He'd order parts and put it all together.

Tonight held unknowns. With any luck, he and this girl would hit it off, and he'd be planning his wedding. His cell phone rang.

"Hoot Owl Hollow. May I help you?" Blake listened to the caller, nodding at intervals. "You think there's a market for this? People will sign up? Mmm. Really? It worked last time?" He scratched his head. Silently he smiled and acknowledged some customers as they came into the shop. "If you can get the people, I don't see why we can't start things up again. Next Wednesday? Sounds fine to me."

Blake smiled. With any luck, his large building might be fully functional after next week. He'd never thought of crafters teaching classes to the public. The space could be divided into sections to accommodate small groups, or several teachers could each take a day and handle a larger group of students. Either way, these ideas were workable.

Later that night, Blake rolled into Gatlinburg, and met Abby's friend, Cindy, at the designated restaurant.

"I'll be wearing a flower clip in my hair," she'd said when they made the date.

Sure enough, she sat waiting for him on a bench located inside the entrance. Blake's heart sank a moment. If he was expecting a look similar to the mysterious woman who bought Devon drinks, he didn't get it.

"Hi, I'm Blake," he said, walking up and shaking her hand.

"I'm Cindy. I don't think we'll have a long wait." Her lips twitched into a nervous smile.

Blake studied her face. Not unattractive, but something about her didn't quite turn him on, either. "Have you ever eaten here before?"

"One time, but that was years ago."

The hostess called out Cindy's last name and led her and Blake to their seat. Blake looked out the window. No calming view of the river. He could use that view right now.

"What do you do, Blake? Abby didn't say much."

"I think Abby keeps a tight lid on things. Holds the cards close to her chest." Blake grinned.

"I guess she didn't tell you that I'm the Maid of Honor for her wedding."

"Huh?" Blake stared at Cindy.

"What's that saying? 'Always a bridesmaid, never a bride.'" She chuckled.

"I've heard that." Blake took a quick sip of his water. He couldn't help but notice the small blemish on the side of her nose, a small raised area not quite fitting the description of a mole or wart. But it was there, nonetheless. He quickly thought of Shorty. If he found out there was any relation, he'd call the whole marriage thing off and be done with it.

One thing he knew right away, he'd have to find date number three. What was the saying? Third time's the charm. Too bad, because this girl wanted to be the bride. He decided he'd make the best of it and enjoy the evening. Cindy seemed like a nice woman. She'd be wonderful for someone. Not him.

***

Eric monitored the sound device while Blake piped away on the flute. The plan included sound recognition so the dancing pig would dance only when someone blew into the tin whistle. The first notes activated the mechanics. More notes would send the pig whirling around on its spindle, including intermittent movements up and down.

All the combined motion looked like the pig was dancing to the whistle. Blake and Eric had reviewed all the mechanics and programming that needed to happen. Eric came up with a list of parts needed, including a programmer who could help with the more intricate workings.

"Aaron can help with some of this, too, I imagine," said Eric.

"He's there if I need him. And the company I'm working with has manufacturers."

"Cool." Eric grinned.

Blake played a little more, and Eric pulled out the flash drive. "Don't lose this, or we'll have to do it all over again. Keep this somewhere safe."

"Will do." Blake took the tiny drive and placed it in his pocket. "You sure I don't owe you a little something for your time?"

"How about another date with my sister?"

"What? Your sister?"

"Cindy. Said she had a good time the other night." Eric tapped Blake on the shoulder. "Great girl. Really likes you a lot."

Blake swallowed hard. "Liked her too." He glanced around the room, feeling Eric's intent gaze burn through him. "I was going to call her tonight, actually."

"No better person than Cindy. Gotta look after my kid sister. You know how that goes." Eric winked.

"Yep, sure do." Blake forced out a laugh, hoping it held some semblance of sincerity. Right now, he wasn't feeling any at all.

Three days later, Blake and Cindy spent the day hiking one of the trails of the Smokies. When no one was looking, Cindy landed a kiss on his lips. Blake felt the hardness grow between his thighs. He could have her. All of her any way he wanted. He knew it. But he couldn't. This charade needed closure at some point, but when? Too delicate to screw up. Too many people involved. Something had to give.

Later that night alone in bed, he reached between his legs and released his pent-up frustration to the tune of crickets and sounds of the night penetrating through his windows. He didn't envision Cindy at all.

***

The rain poured like someone above had dumped barrels of water, and no sign of stopping. Angry black clouds gathered. Blake's mood fell in sync with all of it. Business was slow right now. He'd received an order for a RoundAHerd, but the sale had been his only one since he sold an AutoTrough. No one wanted to get out of their cars in this weather.

The only other people he had on the property were the students and the artisan of the day teaching class in the large building. He charged a rental fee from each crafter who taught, and he allowed the building to be in use seven days a week. Despite that, more money needed to be coming into his business. And he needed a way to kindly end things with Cindy.

He fiddled with the golden pig, inserting the spindle through it so the top touched the bar holding the arms in place.

He had to drill the hole a little wider to accommodate the padding at the top of the spindle. The arm bar needed to rest snugly on it with no danger of any slippage, which meant disaster for the pig. No dancing. The base looked nice for a prototype.

Blake gently slid the pig up and down a little, listening to the tiny clicks as the pointed ends of the legs landed against the top. He spun the pig around. It whirled beautifully, smooth and easy, sparkling in the bright glow of the track lights shining over the checkout counter.

The gold flashes mesmerized him. The momentary quiet of the shop lulled him into a deeper trance. Round and round went the pig. Glints of gold light. Pulsing, warm. See it. Now you don't. There it goes again. Round and round. A light shadow fell over the counter. A presence.

When Blake looked up, he stared into pools of blue swirling from a pair of intent eyes. The look of her nearly got the better of him. When did she come in? He staggered a little to keep from falling down. A twirling lock of blonde hair cascaded down the right side of her face. On the left side, an assortment of tiny flowers mingling in dripping strings of tiny pearls and sparkling crystals. The large pink flower held the remaining hair in a stylish upsweep.

Her red lips glistened with an overlay of thick gloss. Her face radiated like an angel. She studied the pig, watching closely.

"That's really cute," she said.

The sound of her voice sent Blake on high alert. It sounded a lot like the same one he heard when he made his first appointment with Lesander King.

"I kind of think so," said Blake, trying hard to keep from stuttering. "I guess nasty weather didn't keep you from enjoying your day." He smiled, hoping his staring eyes didn't appear too rude. But he couldn't help himself. Hers was a face he could look at for hours and never grow bored.

"I don't let anything keep me from enjoying what I want." Her red lips pulled into a teasing smile.

Blake felt his mouth go dry. He licked his lower lip. "That's good. Can't let things stop you. You'll never get anywhere." His gaze fell on her tattoos. "I really like the artwork of those." He pointed to the area below her neck.

She laughed. "I only got these to bother my dad. He doesn't like them, but I love it. I got the best artist in town."

"Any meaning behind it?"

"Just for show. I like the butterfly because they remind me of freedom. Freedom to be me and do what I want. No one can hold me down."

"Nice philosophy. An even greater way to live it. Just wear it."

Her face sobered. "You look so familiar. I swear I think I've seen you before." The blue in her eyes intensified.

Tell her or not? Blake debated. "I think I've seen you too. Maybe at a bar in Gatlinburg?"

"That's it. I knew it." Another smile lit up her face. "You were with your friend." She leaned on the counter a little. "I guess he was your friend?"

His heart sank. Ugh, why did Devon have to come up? "Yeah, it was me and my friend."

"He's cute. Really nice." The lady nodded.

"You've talked to him?" Blake frowned. The lady seemed too enthusiastic for his taste. Sneaky Devon would never tell him that they had spoken.

"A few times. Seems like a smart guy too."

"He's none too shabby. Nice."

She pointed to the pig. "Where did you get that?"

"I got these . . . from a . . . crafter who works with metals." Blake smiled. He had to come up with a good lie. He didn't want anybody but Aaron to know about his dealing with Lesander King. "He wants to see what else I can do with it."

"Then you must be pretty smart too." The lady rested her elbow on the counter top and looked up at Blake. "I guess you're still working on it." She reached out a slender finger, topped with red nail color that matched her lips, and gently ran it over the golden pig.

Blake's pulse raced as he watched. "You like it?" he asked. With a quick twist, he spun the pig around, watching the lady smile. "You're right, though. I'm not done with it, yet."

"It's really cute." She pulled away from the counter. "Mind if I have a look around?"

"Go right ahead. Can I show you anything in particular?"

"No. I'm fine." The lady walked away to the back of the shop, touching a few items here and there, trying on one of the scarves. She fingered the brightly felted change purses in one of the baskets. In the end, she picked up a jar of body cream and one of the change purses and headed back to the counter. "I'll take these."

"Great choice." Blake rang up the sale on the cash register and took her money, crisp dollar bills. He placed her items in one of his decorative bags and handed it to her. "Hope you enjoy."

"What's your name?" the lady asked, taking the bag.

"Blake. And yours?"

"Avienna."

"Glad you came in, Avienna. Come back any time."

"Good luck with your little pig." She tapped the figurine one last time and slipped out the shop door.

Blake sank down on his stool and closed his eyes. The angel of his dreams had graced his shop with her presence. And on the worst of days with horrid weather. She was just as beautiful close up. He wanted her more than ever. He'd have her. Devon be damned.

"You-hoo. I brought you something." A woman's voice chirped out.

He turned and saw Cindy stepping through the door, water dripping off a bright chintzy floral rain slicker. His face reddened.

"Brought you some lunch. Thought you might be hungry." Cindy smiled and placed a bag on the counter.

"You didn't have to get out in this weather. It's dangerous out there." Blake helped remove Cindy's slicker and hung it on a coat rack in a corner behind the counter.

"Nothing's too much trouble for you." She wrapped her arms around Blake's neck and kissed him. "You having a good day, even if it is crappy weather?"

"Mmm." Blake nodded and smiled. His guilt had increased ten-fold.

"What's up for the weekend? Anything fun in mind?" she asked.

"Don't know. Haven't thought about it."

He really needed to think about it.

***

The rain had stopped. By the time the shop closed, the sun had peeked out from the clouds a little. Twilight was setting in, and he only had short time before night blanketed everything. In his hand, he held one of the crisp bills Avienna had given him when she paid for her purchases earlier.

An owl let out a mournful "Whoo-whoo. Whooo." A light breeze rustled through the trees. The rush of water sounded clearer and more emphatic as Blake reached the river. He gazed out across the currents, eyeing the swirls of chilly water whirling downstream. Why had he not made time to come sit here after work?

Even Cindy hadn't seen this area of his property. Not yet. After meeting Avienna today, maybe not ever. He hadn't made any attempts to get closer to Cindy, no fondling, and definitely no full love-making. Kissing was about as far as he'd gone. She hadn't pushed much further than that, either. For that, he counted his lucky stars. But an unspoken longing in her eyes haunted him at times.

Blake stared up at the sky a moment. He didn't believe in magic or superstition, and why he'd brought the dollar bill with him this evening to the river perplexed him more. But he came with an intent, an intent that burned strong within him. The desire for Avienna pulled at him to such a degree that he was willing to go any route to get her.

If this meant wishing upon a star or making a wish in one form or another, he'd do it. The money held a connection to her, something she'd touched, owned. If he sent it back to nature and the universe, would she come back to him? Blake took the bill, folded it tightly, and made his wish. He even spoke it aloud for good measure.

When he finished verbalizing his desire, Blake tossed the bill, watching it sail through the air and into the rushing currents of the river. He barely saw where it landed. In an instant, the money disappeared. Whether it sank to the bottom immediately or floated down stream, carried on the crests of rushing water, he'd never know. It didn't matter. All that mattered was Avienna's return.

***

In one of the largest chalet homes perched on a solid cliff overlooking Gatlinburg, Avienna sat curled up gazing out one of the large picture windows. The lights in the valley twinkled as if a fairy had tossed magical sprinkle dust over the small town and the main strip that flowed with the life blood of tourists and locals alike.

She'd lived here all her life. A sleepy little town with humble pioneer origins had transformed into a bustling attraction for people nationwide. Retail made the town, and she knew it. Her father knew it.

Alcohol and t-shirts flowed, endless as the rivers rushing by. But her family wanted to contribute more, works of beauty, enchanting and unique. Art that would leave a mark on the owner's soul, something unforgettable. Pieces that could be passed on with pride.

Something else had awakened her, and it wasn't an astounding blow to the senses, but a gentle nudge. Powerful, nonetheless. The guy behind the checkout counter seemed more than nice. Attractive, smooth voice. Smart. What would he really end up doing with that darling golden piglet? What was he like when he wasn't working?

His friend had not made a move to ask her out or see her outside the bar. She had made the first move with smiles, nods, and purchasing him a drink each time they met, her way of showing her interest. Nothing. Avienna liked Devon. He was who she really wanted.

True to her old-fashioned leanings, she preferred the man taking the lead. In her mind, men were slower in catching up to women when it came to admitting emotions of interest or love. Many people may laugh at her or strongly disagree, but in her experience, this was a fact. A man could be intelligent and strong, but waffling on love was a huge no-no.

The lack of action had frustrated her a great deal. She either had to go against her own grain and ask him out or move on. There was his friend, but her interest in Devon had likely ruined any chance of the man in the store taking a lead. He already knew she didn't have him on her radar. His gaze haunted her. Penetrating eyes and a face that held a strong spark of interest.

It was there. She had seen it, felt it. Did she want to shift gears, focus on someone else? Already in her mid-twenties, life was passing her by. The bar scenes were getting old, and she didn't care about being alone anymore.

"What's my girl brooding about?" Lesander King wandered in the room and sat down by his daughter. "You're thinking hard about something. Enjoy your day off?"

"I'm good." Avienna smiled and rested her head briefly on her father's shoulder. "The view is so pretty out there."

"Why are you not out there in it with your friends? Everyone busy?"

"Don't know. Guess I didn't feel much like going out tonight." She turned her gaze back to the window.

"What do you want, Avienna? You're a big help in the office, but is it really what you want to do?"

"It's fine. No problem with it, whatsoever."

Lesander King angled his head sideways a little, studying his daughter. "What sets your heart on fire? What do you really want more than anything?"

Avienna didn't say anything at first, keeping her eyes focused on the lights in the distance.

"Oh, come on, honey." King rubbed his daughter's shoulder. "I'm glad you like taking part in the business, but I think you're wanting more, or at least something to go along with it."

"I'd like to find the one meant for me." Avienna faced her father. "I think I'm outgrowing all the running around with girlfriends and dealing with the wrong man. I want the right one."

Lesander smiled. "Then go after the right one. Put yourself in the company of where the right one would most likely hang out." He whispered in her ear, "I'll give you a hint. Bars aren't the place."

Avienna grinned and kissed her father on the cheek. "I think you're right about that."

***

Devon sat rocking with Blake on the front porch at Hoot Owl Hollow. Both nursed frosty cold bottles of beer and munched on hot deli sandwiches Devon had brought for dinner.

"So what's the news you're wanting to tell me?" Blake asked. He lifted his beer for a sip.

"I'm interviewing with Lesander King tomorrow."

Blake's heart nearly stopped at the announcement. The beer bottle in his mouth helped him at least keep a steady face. He swallowed and nodded. "Nice. How did you hear about him?"

"Like you don't know?"

Blake frowned. "What's that supposed to mean?"

"You know exactly who Lesander King is. So don't act so surprised." Devon arched an eyebrow, keeping his tone steady and more teasing than antagonizing.

"My question stands. How did you hear about him?"

"Let's just say I have my connections."

"Okay. What are you wanting from the interview, then?"

"I want a shot at something different, big. Just like you." Devon's gaze landed squarely on Blake's eyes.

The conversation frustrated Blake.

Had Aaron also shared the letter with Devon, at some point? It's not like Aaron had to be a hundred percent loyal to any one person. Devon and Abby attended his classes along with many others who were paying students at the university. He had been nothing more than a charity case. Still, the fact Devon would soon have his foot in the door toward a position in Lesander King's company unnerved him.

"What will you tell him?" asked Blake.

"He'll learn about everything I've created and worked on. Got my resumé ready to go." Devon smiled at Blake. "What was he like when you went? Is he pretty laid back or easy to talk to? Or is he a tough old cuss?"

"Don't know, man." Blake shook his head and continued eating.

Devon studied his friend in silence for several seconds. He put is food down and asked. "Will there ever be time when we end this unsaid competition between us?"

Blake tilted his head, displaying a perplexed look. "You think we constantly compete? Is that what keeps you up at night?"

"I sleep fine. And by the way, my admirer bought me another drink the other night."

The comment was a clear jab. Blake knew it. He kept up his poker face. "That's great. Good for you."

Blake knew this battle wasn't over, but he hoped with every fiber of his being that Avienna wouldn't mention coming to his shop. Devon didn't say anything about that, and he wondered if his friend wasn't bluffing him into talking. He'd never give in.

Devon broke the silence. "Things okay with you and Cindy? She's really into you." He arched an eyebrow, grinning. "That's what I hear from Abby."

"She's all right. We hike, go out." Blake leveled his gaze at Devon. Words needed careful choosing. Everything he said could be taken straight to Avienna, if Devon talked to her at all.

"You two getting serious?" Devon's eyes narrowed.

"Are you?" Blake couldn't resist. He didn't want to come right out and ask, but his tongue loosened before he could stop it.

"What?"

"You know exactly what I'm asking you." Blake's eyes lit up.

Devon lowered his gaze, focusing on his food. He didn't answer.

Blake cursed silently to himself. He was going solo on this deal where Avienna was concerned. Devon wasn't talking, and he didn't know how tight-lipped she might be. Kept him guessing. It also put him in a position of having to play his cards carefully. Avienna was destined to be his. Period.

He'd set his intent and made the wish. If she saw Devon as smart and cute, how would he battle against that and win her over?

"Eric asked me to be best man," Devon spoke up. "Did I tell you that, already?"

"News to me. Congrats, man."

"I thought that was okay." Devon nodded.

"You'll be walking Cindy down the aisle."

Devon pressed his lips together, considering Blake's statement. "True."

"Does all that make you feel weird?"

"Like how?"

Blake laughed. "You know, hitting close to home. It could be you tying the knot."

"Or it could be you. With Cindy. Do you ever think about that?" Devon stared at his friend.

"I'm like you. I take it nice and slow." Blake returned the stare.

The two men finished their meals to the sound of birds, crickets—and the sound of Cindy's car pulling up behind Blake's.

Chapter Nine

Blake wiggled the spindle into the tiny hole on the base. After placing all the mechanical parts underneath, including an audio chip, a first dancing pig was finished. It looked good on the outside, but would it work the way it should?

There were customers in the shop, so Blake couldn't test his invention right away. When Cindy brought lunch, that delayed him more. She stayed longer than usual, chatting and waiting on customers like she owned the place. Blake watched with mild interest as she moved around the store, all smiles.

She'd taken the liberty to check out other potential lines he could carry in the shop. One artisan had halted classes, so she contacted a friend of a friend to see if the they could fill the empty day with a new craft students could learn. Blake rang everyone up at the cash register, thankful for the sales.

"Looks like things are going really well for you now." Cindy sidled up to Blake, smiling up at him. "Your new teacher will be ready to start in two weeks, so you'll have a full schedule again."

"You're too good, Cindy." Blake hugged her. "You like this place, don't you?"

"I like helping you. It's fun." She stared into his eyes. The expression on her face changed. The grin had faded, and in its place, a questioning look. "Do you like it when I help, or is it over-stepping my bounds?" Cindy seemed nervous all of a sudden. Her eyes darted from the shelves at the other end of the store back to his face.

Blake didn't like the feeling of his stomach tightening up. She had something on her mind, and he didn't want to hear it. "No. You're fine. Really. Love having you here."

They were alone in the shop now. He wished more than anything that some customers would come in.

"How about if I helped you all the time? Maybe help you come up with some of your new projects? I could come after classes and on weekends."

The suggestions stunned him. Worse, it put him on the spot.

"You're trying to get through school, studying. There's no time to help me. I'm good right now."

She pulled away from him, pretending to re-arrange some of the items on the shelf. "That's fine. Just thought I'd ask." She forced a light chuckle. "If you change your mind let me know. I'm good at multi-tasking. And sometimes I need a break. You know how some of those engineering classes can be kind of dry."

"How well I know." Blake laughed. "If you ever need a break, I'm here." He cleared his throat and looked quickly out the window. Where were customers when you needed them? Plenty of cars drove by. Why didn't one or two of them stop?

"Why haven't you asked me to spend the night with you?" Cindy turned around and faced Blake, staring into his face. "We've been going out a while. I'm just wondering, that's all." Despite the confrontative nature of the question, the expression on her face showed the look of someone deeply hurt rather than angry.

Where were the customers? C'mon, customers. Don't let me down. Blake prayed silently to himself. But no amount of praying brought anyone through the door.

"I like to take my time in relationships, see how things go." Blake swallowed hard. Really? How true was that? He may not have been the alpha stud like some of the younger men in his father's business, but he had moved pretty fast on a couple of previous girlfriends. Was it pure lust, or had it been simple immaturity? Maybe lust and immaturity.

Cindy crossed her arms, staring at him.

"Look," said Blake, fumbling for words. "I respect you, and I don't want to move too fast. That's all." He stepped out from behind the counter and wrapped an arm around her. "Aw, Cindy. We have time. May not feel like it, but we do."

No, he didn't have time, and he cursed himself even more for not going on some dates while living at Calin's place. A date every now and then might have solved his problem. Once his studies kicked in, the golden box had been forgotten. He regretted that now.

"I see." Cindy pulled away. She grabbed her purse and pulled out a cell phone. Her eyes widened when she viewed the screen. "I gotta run. One of my friends needs me to come her way." She smiled. "Hope you make more sales. Call me later, if you get time." Quickly, she slipped out the front door.

Blake let out a sigh and shook his head. Never mind the fact that he'd caught a quick glimpse of Cindy's phone and saw no notices lighting up the screen nor heard a message ding from the phone. His heart hurt. It hurt for her and for him. The door opened and several customers came through.

Five minutes before closing time, he picked up the tin whistle. He piped out a few notes, keeping his eye on the tiny golden pig. To his relief, it whirled round and round. The mechanics had kicked in, adding the up and down motion in between a couple of spins. Blake tooted some more on the whistle.

"You've got it working."

Startled, Blake glanced up and stopped blowing. The little pig spun one last time and landed on the tip of its toes.

"Do it again. I want to see it." Avienna's eyes lit up.

Blake blew into the whistle. The pig whirled around clock-wise, lifted up on its toes twice, and spun around counter clock-wise. The longer the sounds trailed out, the more the pig kept dancing. Round and round, lift, lift, round and round the other way.

Avienna walked closer to the counter, eyes sparkling. "That's the cutest thing I've ever seen. I liked the idea when I saw it last time. I love it better now."

"Turned out pretty good, if I say so myself." Blake laid the whistle aside, staring into her face. "To what do I owe this pleasure of seeing you again?"

"Wanted to get out a little. Take a drive through the woods."

"Bored?"

She didn't answer, but smiled and turned away, heading for the back shelves. "I liked that body cream I got here last time. Might buy something else to go with it."

"There's a lip balm in that line." Blake stepped out from behind the counter and walked toward Avienna. "It makes your lips kissably soft like the cream makes your skin caressably soft."

The two stared at each other. Avienna's lips twitched into a light smile.

"You know that for sure?" she asked in a sultry voice.

Her tone set Blake nearly on fire. Heat rose to his face, and he fought to keep the stiffness inside his jeans in check.

"I know quite a bit—for sure." He smiled back.

Avienna squared up her shoulders, the smile remaining on her glistening red lips. Her words came out barely audible, more sensual than before. "Anyone who can make a sweet golden pig dance probably knows quite a bit." She winked.

Blake watched through narrowed eyes as she plucked off a sealed tube of lip balm. He quickly adjusted his jeans before she turned around.

"I'll take some hand cream too. I guess they make your hands silky soft for that caressable skin?"

"Every bit," Blake murmured close to her ear. He stepped back, acutely aware of their closeness.

Her cheeks flushed. The look enhanced her beauty, bringing out the porcelain sheen of her skin, turning up the light in her eyes. Her entire attention focused on him, and he knew it.

"Shall I take these up front and let you look around some more?" Blake took the two items from her hands, brushing his fingers against hers.

The young woman blinked like someone waking from a state of daydreaming. She licked her lower lip, watching Blake walk back to the counter. After few minutes of feigned interest in shopping, Avienna headed back up front.

"I guess that's all for today." Her demeanor had changed. Her face showed a deep hunger brewing inside. An inner longing she wished to keep hidden in one respect, but desired to express if given a chance.

Blake sensed it, felt it as strongly as she did. He knew what he wanted; she did, too, whether she'd admit it or not.

"Sure you don't want anything else?" He scribbled in the ticket book.

"Yeah. I'm good for now." Her voice came out a little hoarse. She rubbed a hand over the side of her neck and looked around briefly. Her gaze fell on the golden pig. "Can you play one more time so I can see it dance again? Just once before I go home?"

"Sure." He finished up the order, took her money, and picked up the whistle.

The tiny piglet whirled and lifted on tiptoe while Blake tooted on the instrument. Avienna watched in fascination, eyes glittering with excitement. When Blake stopped, the pig slowed down, resting its tiny pointed toes on the base.

"How much do you want for it?" she asked.

He pulled the whistle away from his mouth. "What?"

"How much? I want to buy him."

Blake's eyes widened. "He's not for sale."

Her face clouded. "Why not? It works fine."

"It's only a prototype for a special project I'm working on." Blake's heart pounded. The last thing he wanted was to argue with the woman of his dreams. Over a pig.

"So? It doesn't look like a prototype."

Blake and Avienna stood in silence, their eyes darting back and forth from the piglet to each other.

"I want him," whispered Avienna.

"I can't sell him to you. He's really not mine to sell."

"You got more?"

"Mmm, I may have some more." Blake turned his gaze to the ceiling and back to the woman's eyes.

"What do I have to do before I can take this pig home with me tonight?"

Avienna meant business. Blake stared into two pools of flashing blue determination. Her red lips, pursed together in defiance, turned him on. Blake didn't know what had hit him, whether the suggestive banter earlier at the shelves had riled everything up, or he at once saw a way to strike out for the woman of his dreams.

"What will you do, Avienna, to take this pig home with you tonight?"

She stared him squarely in the eyes and whispered, "I'll do anything."

Blake's eyebrows shot up. "Really? Anything?"

"Anything."

"Where do you draw the line?" He couldn't resist asking.

"What do you mean?"

"What's the limit? I could ask you to do something you may not exactly like. But would you do it, anyway?" He grinned.

She leaned away from the counter. "Maybe?" Her lips spread into smile. The light in her eyes burned brighter. Her breath quickened slightly.

"Come with me to my cabin." Blake stood up straighter than ever, keeping his eyes fixed in her direction.

Avienna scowled. "Your cabin? Isn't money good enough?" She grinned. "I'll pay you whatever you want."

"I don't want your money." Blake tapped gently on the little gold pig. "You want this, you do what I ask."

The young woman stood a moment, thinking, considering his proposal. Blake tried keeping calm and holding his own. He had this. If luck were on his side, he'd have her all to himself within minutes.

"I'll do what you ask, but it has to be limited, whatever it is. You can't go hog wild and pig crazy. Know what I mean?" She tilted her head, eyeing him with an intent look.

He laughed. "Deal. Let me lock up, and we'll go."

***

Blake opened the door of the cabin and motioned for Avienna to go inside. Her eyes lit up as she looked around. He placed the pig on the kitchen table.

"This place is cute. I love it. It's like something out of a fairy tale."

"It has its charm. The bedroom is this way." Blake escorted her into his room. Though they were completely alone, he shut the door anyway.

"Why do things always have to involve . . .? She let out a sigh.

"Why not? You have something against that?" Blake cocked an eyebrow. "Why do some people think time in the bedroom is bad?"

"Oh, it's not. It's just . . . I mean . . ." She turned around directly in front of him. "You only get one choice of what you want to do, and it can't be all the way, if you know what I mean. That's not an option."

"But you said you'd do anything. It's for the pig. You really like it."

"I can also decide I don't want the pig anymore." Her lips pulled into a one-sided grin.

Blake moved in closer, wrapping his arms around her. "But you want that little piggy so much." His voice lowered. "There's nothing else in the world like him."

"What do you want to do? Make your choice."

"I want to see your breasts." His lips brushed against her ear.

"That's all you'll see."

He watched her unbutton the blouse, but she didn't take it off. Blake decided he wouldn't press too much. The proposition enough was bold beyond imagination. And she'd accepted. She revealed a Victorian-style bustier, which fascinated him to the highest degree.

"Fancy lingerie," he said.

"Keeps everything in place better than bras."

The two fell silent. All Blake heard was Avienna unhooking the undergarment. She opened both sides, baring a set of tantalizing breasts topped with pert, succulent nipples.

Blake eyed her with brazen lust. He pulled her close, studying every inch, every detail, tracing a finger around her curves. She closed her eyes and sucked in her breath.

"How long has it been since you've been touched, Avienna?" he murmured.

"A long time. Despite what you might think of me right now, I'm pretty picky about men."

He spoke into her ear, "I think you're beautiful." Without another word, he lowered his head toward one of her breasts and flicked out his tongue.

She let out a moan. He felt her tense in his arms, but she didn't fight or push away. Given this permission, Blake licked the nipple, running his tongue around the tip, allowing himself the pleasure of feeling his flesh on hers. He suckled her, gently at first. His urgency grew, and he sucked harder, ending with a soft bite.

Avienna cried out, but not too loudly. Blake pleasured himself the same way with her other breast. For several minutes, he treated himself, licking, sucking, fondling with his fingers, squeezing. She allowed him the time he wanted, the time he needed.

"I think you've earned yourself a golden pig." Blake pulled away, allowing her to hook the bodice back in place.

When they left Blake's room, he headed to the kitchen table and handed her the pig. "All for you."

She cradled the pig gently in one hand, opening the door with the other. Without a word, Avienna left. Blake listened to the roar of her car engine starting. Outside the window, he watched the vehicle turn onto Rapid Rivers Road and head off to the frenetic energy of the Gatlinburg strip.

The ache between Blake's legs throbbed without mercy, driving him mad if he didn't do something about it. He ran to his bedroom and stripped. Stepping into a running shower, he closed his eyes, losing himself in the lukewarm water streaming over his back. With one hand between his thighs, he worked himself to a peak of ecstasy, holding fast the vision of Avienna in his mind.

His fingers rubbed over and tugged at a swollen cock. When he couldn't handle anymore, he let out a grunt. The release of pent-up lust sent a heated wave radiating through him, and he backed against the cold tile wall, heart pounding hard in his chest. One thing he knew. He was tired of jacking off alone.

If he played his cards right, he wouldn't have to worry about it anymore.

Blake shook his head, clearing the fog from a set of blurry eyes. He smiled. She'd be back. Maybe not, if she held a grudge. But a good, solid maybe lay in his favor.

***

Avienna stared at the pig, scowling. "Why won't you dance, dammit?" She'd tried everything, from playing music on her cell phone, to solo flute music on Spotify. When those options didn't work, she whistled and sung to the pig. It just stood there, motionless. A cute, golden, stubborn little figurine. "I should have known he'd do this. Sneaky thing. And over-sexed too." She let out a sharp sound of anguish and rested her head against her hand.

She jumped when someone knocked at the door. Quick, she had to hide the pig. Didn't know why, exactly, but something compelled her to do it. Avienna jerked open a drawer in her desk and carefully put the pig inside. "Come in."

"What are you doing in here?" Lesander stepped into the room, grinning. "I heard you yelling all the way out there." He pointed to the door.

"Sorry, Dad. I was working on something."

"Like what? I never see you working on anything."

Her mouth dropped open in indignation. "That's not true!"

Lesander King laughed. "Were you working on a special project for me? Something we can make some money selling?" He kissed the top of her head. "You're as smart as the rest of them, Avi. Good creativity always works. Anything else lacking can be done by someone else."

Avienna shook her head. "Not right now, but I do give some thought to the business, though."

"I have one of my interviewees working on a special project, but I haven't heard back from him yet. He has a little time left."

"Ohh, what is it?" Her eyes brightened.

Her father placed a finger over his lips. "My secret. Not telling."

She grimaced. "Let me see it when it's finished."

"Will do. It should be rather unique." He smiled and left the room.

When the door shut, Avienna opened the drawer and studied the piglet some more, inspecting the base, top and bottom. There was little to the design. Only an opening that apparently captured the sound of . . . the flute! Now she knew the problem. The pig only danced to one type of sound. Sneaky, sexy Blake didn't give her the flute to go with the pig.

Sneaky, sexy. Definitely sexy. Avienna clapped a hand over her mouth. She had to stop thinking of him that way, but it was too late now. His friend had always lingered in the back of her mind—before she met Blake personally that fateful day when first ambling into his store.

The more she thought about the moment in his bedroom, the harder her clit hammered. So hard it hurt. Feeling him touch her intimately had filled her body with a heady, vibrant energy she hadn't enjoyed in a long time. In a grip of pleasure-pain, she jumped up from the desk, locked her bedroom door, and lay down on her bed.

Sliding her hand inside her jeans, Avienna aimed for the knot of sensitive nerves pounding between her legs. She landed a sure finger on it and rubbed. Slowly, faster, slow again, up and down, round and round. The whole time she replayed the images and sensations of Blake sucking on her nipples and squeezing her breasts.

She was on a precipice, waiting to drown in an explosion of pure bliss. One more round with her finger and her body erupted in a wave of spasms, hard, rhythmic, delicious. Her thighs quivered; she bucked with pleasure. One good, hard orgasm wasn't enough. She pleasured herself a few more times, losing herself in heated contractions, delighting in feeling a swollen clit pressed against her finger. When she finished, Avienna calmed her breathing. The wetness between her legs trickled slowly down. "That felt so good," she whispered softly.

***

Later that night, Blake and Cindy sat together at a popular restaurant at the far end of the Gatlinburg strip. He hated this date with a passion he couldn't put into words. As much as being with Avienna had thrilled him, this night with Cindy hurt him to the core. Her face beamed at him as they sipped wine and waited on their order.

They had already made a trip to the salad bar. He'd pull out the stops on spending and told her to order the best steak on the menu. When they finished they'd have dessert. They enjoyed their meal when the server brought their food. Cindy was chattering away, talking about the shop, her classes. The two of them.

Blake listened, cringing inside. The lady sitting across from him indicated she had hopes for a bright future, one including him in it. When the dishes had been cleared away and fresh cups of coffee and dessert placed before them, he sat up straight and reached for her hand.

"Cindy, we need to talk . . ."

Chapter Ten

The balmy night air did little to console Blake. A starry night didn't soothe him, either. He sat on the porch of his cabin gazing out into the dark, sipping a small tumbler of straight whiskey. How would Abby and Eric take it when they found out? While he rocked, the events of the night played over and over.

A woman who had planned on enjoying a romantic night with her beloved, entertaining a blissful future with a happily ever after, left the restaurant in a flood of tears. Alone at the table, Blake sat with only dreams of Avienna keeping him momentarily sane. He'd gone a little too far. Maybe he should have ended the relationship with Cindy soon after they met, but he'd hung on, hoping for a change in heart.

His only consolation, not sleeping with her. He vowed from the beginning he wouldn't do it unless he was totally and completely sure of his feelings, that he loved her. She'd make a fantastic wife for the right person. At least she didn't have time constraints like he did. Blake counted the time left before he could kiss the golden box goodbye.

***

Bright and early, Blake arose from a fitful sleep and headed to the large building where he spent the morning creating a new dancing pig. He'd ordered all the parts. He needed a prototype to take to Lesander King. With his approval, he'd land himself a handy position allowing him to come up with a host of unique items that had a ready market.

Blake selected another golden pig from the box and prepared it like he did for the first one. The process went much faster than before. By the time he opened the shop, he at least had the holes drilled and the arms bent in place and filed. He took the rest of the parts with him to the shop.

The moment he opened the doors, people came in immediately. It wasn't until the last hour before closing time that he had some time to work on the pig in between waiting on customers. When six o'clock rolled around, someone stepped into the shop.

Blake looked up. Sight of the visitor sent a bad feeling crawling all over him.

"Hey, Abby. What brings you here?" He placed the pig and other parts aside on the counter.

"I really need to talk to you." she said. A light smile covered her face.

"Look, I'm really sorry about—"

She shook her head. "If you're about to close the doors, can we go for a walk afterward, maybe to the river?"

"Sure. We can do that." The request made Blake even more nervous. Did she want to tell him off in a place where no one had a chance to hear? He flipped out the lights, placed the Closed sign on the door, and led the way to the river.

Abby stood looking over it in silence, taking in the view. The breeze blew through her hair and the late evening sun lit up her face. Blake still wondered at the beauty of this woman. He sauntered up to her near the river's edge and stood by her quietly.

"Cindy told me what happened." Abby at last turned around and faced Blake.

"I'm really sorry." He swiped at his hair, nervous. The late-summer heat seemed extra warm right now. His being pinned for a discussion on a break-up made everything worse.

"What's wrong with you, Blake?" Abby's eyes held a flash of indignation.

"Huh?"

"You heard me. What's wrong with you? I fixed you up with two nice friends. I'll accept the fact that the first one didn't quite flow. But Cindy? She's everything. And she liked you so much."

Blake stared out over the water.

"She feels led on, you know. Who was it you met? I want to know."

"I can't go into that." Blake shook his head.

"Why not? What's the big secret?" Abby's faced had clouded with irritation. "Look, I helped you because of this stupid time-frame you've put yourself on, and you dump a nice girl who's really interested in you for someone new. Someone who may toss you aside like you did Cindy."

Blake winced at the words. "I am willing to let that golden box go if I have to. I won't just rush into something. But if I could pull it off . . ." Blake wagged his head from side to side, trying to emphasize his point.

"I'm not helping you find true love anymore." Abby placed her hand on his arm. "You're on your own. Won't have my friends hurt. And I know the first one wasn't interested, so I don't blame you entirely for that loss."

"I know, Abby. And again, I'm sorry. Maybe I need to just let it go. What happens happens."

"Can we change the subject and let me talk to you about having my wedding here?"

"You still plan on doing that? I thought you'd be mad enough to not go through with it." Blake gauged her emotions closely.

"I'm not happy with what's happened, but I have my life, and I intend on marrying Eric. I'd like to do it here with my family and best friends watching."

"I'll make sure your wedding is a success as far as location goes. That's the best I can do."

"That's all I expect from you. Surely you won't mess up a location." Her face showed a mock frown, which relieved Blake somewhat. Maybe she'd forgive him someday.

"Tell you what, I'll go so far as to map out places that would make great shots for the photographer, spots where you could have the ceremony. I'll suggest places where you could set up a tent for the reception, if you want to consider having your reception here too."

Abby's eyes lit up. "A reception would be great. I'd love Gatlinburg, but that can get so crowded and hectic. It's beautiful out here."

"You'll have everything next week. I know you're on a time crunch."

"Blake, are you sure you can't talk to me about the new woman you've met? I'm dying to hear about her." She looked sideways at him.

"I really can't. Not right now."

"Is she worth it? Worth choosing over Cindy?"

"If this works out, she'll be worth it." Blake nodded, gazing at Abby. "Yeah, she'll be worth it."

***

Avienna drove straight to Hoot Owl Hollow. Two weeks had passed. Due to a hectic schedule, getting out to Rapid Rivers Road had taken a back seat on her calendar. He'd be closing soon, and she wanted him to make it right. She wanted a golden dancing pig. Blake owed it to her. This time the owner behind the counter better make good and sure everything was together, flute and all.

When a customer pulled out, she whipped into the spot and turned off the engine. Her cell phone clock showed five minutes more to go before he closed up for the night. Time for sneaky, sexy Blake to make good on his promise of giving her what she wanted.

Why couldn't his friend have been more like him, at least ask her out when they saw each other at the bar—more than once? After the intimate moment with Blake, Avienna had not returned to the bar. The humble store owner had awakened her. Something about him tempted her now, an irresistible charm she had missed the first time on seeing the two friends. When she stepped inside the shop and landed her vision on his smile, her heart skipped a beat.

"Missed me?" Blake grinned.

Avienna held her own, trying not to be too smitten by the sparkle in his eyes.

"You sent me home with a defective pig. How could you do that?" She glanced around the store, confirming they were completely alone. "We had a deal."

"It was a sweet deal, if I remember," said Blake. "I hope you found it as sweet as I did?"

"You knew good and well that pig wouldn't dance without the flute. Was it that easy for you to forget? The piece that made everything work?"

Blake remained behind the counter, staring her in the face. He quickly licked his lower lip.

"Well?" She pressed against the counter, leaning her upper body toward him.

He leaned over toward her, so close their noses nearly touched. "People make mistakes. I simply forgot, that's all."

"Do you have another one? I want it." Avienna stepped back, rapping her fingers on the counter for emphasis.

"I happen to have another one. Just finished it today."

"Good. Can you put it in a bag so I can take it home?"

"Not so fast. Sure, I made a boo-boo and forgot the flute, but that doesn't mean I can just up and give you a pig for nothing." Blake narrowed his eyes at her.

Avienna wrinkled her brow. "Why not? It was your boo-boo."

"Doesn't matter. You want this pig? There is a price for it."

"What do you want now?" Her two eyes gleamed from a face turning a light pink.

He smiled. "I'm closing up now. This pig goes home with you if you come home with me."

"Again?" She pouted to his face, but inside, her heart raced. A wave of heat washed over her. What would he have in mind this time?

"Yes. You ready?" Without another word, Blake cut off the lights and locked up the shop.

He led the way down the path to the cabin, carrying the pig and flute in a bag. After placing the figurine on the table, he guided Avienna back to his bedroom.

"Just be decent, whatever it is you want." Her eyes flashed.

"I hope I was more than decent last time. If I remember, you seemed to think I was pretty good." He clucked his tongue at the memory, grinning.

Her cheeks flushed scarlet. "It was . . . good."

"Just good?" Blake scratched his head. "Hmm. Well, this time it has to be more than good." He whispered in her ear. "This time has to be a moment you'll never forget. Ever." The last word came out with emphasis. "I'm guessing that the fancy Victorian bustier you wore last time has to have some garters with it. I mean, what would go with a sexy bustier? Garters, right?"

Avienna flinched, excited. "Maybe."

"I want to see if I'm right." Blake led her to the bed. "If I'm right, I get to do what I want again. I'll keep it simple, though."

"Fine." She glanced around the room, hesitating.

"Don't stop. Keep going. I want to see if I'm right."

She pulled at the cotton skirt she wore and timidly lifted it up, inch by inch.

"You're such a tease," Blake murmured, pleased with the way things were going.

The corner of Avienna's mouth lifted up into a half-grin. "I'm really not a tease. But you go ahead and think anything you want."

When the skirt reached the upper part of her thighs, a set of garters came into view. Blake held his breath. A set of silk stockings covered a pair of shapely legs.

"Nice. You're almost done."

"What do you want me to do now?" she asked.

"Undo those garters and lay on the bed. After that, I take over."

Her eyes widened. "Are you serious?"

"As serious as you are about taking a pig home." Blake rubbed his chin, meeting her gaze.

Avienna did as instructed, unhooking the stocking on each leg. Slowly she eased herself on the bed.

"Don't bother smoothing your skirt down and acting all prim and proper. That'll be a waste of time." Blake grinned. "Lay back and relax, nice and easy."

The way he commanded sent her mind in a whirl. Already a pool of wetness had gathered between her legs. This man knew how to take charge. Had she ever asked how he learned about fashioning golden pigs that could dance to the sound of a flute? She couldn't remember. What else had this man done in his life? One thing dawned on her. Blake was more than a simple shop owner.

Of course, they hadn't spent that much time together, but he somehow transcended that fact, making what time they did spend together memorable beyond her wildest dreams. It all made an indelible impression on her mind. Avienna wouldn't forget it if she lived a hundred years.

Blake climbed onto the bed. Carefully, he removed the stockings, stroking the insides of her thighs as he did so. Avienna's breath hitched in her throat. In a stunning move, he hooked two fingers from each hand around her lace bikini-style panties and pulled them off. She sat up a moment, mouth open in protest.

"Shh. Lay back down or no pig for you." His voice came out in a sing-song, teasing tone.

She did as he instructed. Having removed her undergarments could mean only one thing. This romantic round would be much more involved than the last one.

Their eyes met. Avienna watched him lower his head below her hips. She held her breath for what would come next. Blake tenderly spread her open, landed the tip of his tongue on her aching clit, and licked with a series of circular motions intermixed with up and down. When he finished with that, he sucked gently.

Avienna let out an involuntary moan. She couldn't hold back. His tongue played a merciless, delectable number on her. The hot bundle of nerves at the top of her sex throbbed harder than ever. His tongue traced over all her parts, finding a curve, then another. When he reached her entrance, he worked his tongue inside as far as it would go, swirling and pushing.

One last round on her clit, licking and sucking, and she let out a small shout. A wave of spasms washed over her, sending her hips jerking and shuddering. Blake slipped two fingers deep inside of her, turning them up and moving in forward and backward motions. The movement hit her G-spot. Avienna thought she'd slipped into another dimension.

Blake watched with a gleam in his eyes. "Was this better than good?"

Her reply came out as a simple moan.

"Get dressed. I'll give you the pig."

He waited in the kitchen. When she came out, he handed her the bag with the flute and pig. She stared at him a moment. More than anything she wanted to kiss him but didn't want to appear any more eager than she may already have.

What interested her at the moment was the bulge she noted in his jeans. Her fingers twitched. He'd be fun to play with, stroke, suck. It wasn't happening today, though. Taking the bag in her hands, she rushed out the door, headed to her car, and sped off.

Blake leaned against the kitchen wall and closed his eyes, smiling to himself. The pig may have appeared complete and ready for operation, but no deal. The sound chip hadn't been installed, yet. No matter how much Avienna played, that pig wouldn't dance, either. With thoughts of their recent interlude moments earlier, he reached inside his jeans, toyed with his swollen cock, and jerked himself off. Would she ever forget completely about Devon and truly want only him?

***

"I love all the spots you selected." Abby shielded her eyes from the sun and gazed back toward the river. "You've got some great locations here."

"I think a good photographer will make it all come out even better." Blake smiled, and handed her a hand-drawn map of his property. "Here you go. You'll have something so you can plan better."

Abby lightly punched Blake's arm. "Only three weeks away before the big day."

"You really love him?"

"I think we fell in love the day we first met." She laughed. "I don't believe in love at first sight, but it seemed to happen to us. What about you?"

Blake thought a moment. "I think I do believe in love at first sight." He turned and gazed into Abby's face. "I only say that because I think two people can have an immediate reaction to each other for some reason. Maybe there is such a thing as soul attraction." He shook his head. "Don't know."

"You still seeing that girl you dumped Cindy for?"

"Are you going to rub my nose in it forever?" Blake sensed a small twinge of annoyance welling up.

"Not forever, but for a little while." Abby looked at him, grinning. "After the wedding, I'll stop."

"Has she found anyone else?" He sincerely hoped so.

"She and Devon have been talking some. I don't know about what."

"Maybe they have something big planned for the wedding or reception?"

Abby tapped Blake's shoulder. "You didn't answer my question."

"Yeah, saw her the other day, as a matter of fact."

"Tick tock, Blake. I hope it all works out. And fast."

***

Time for the moment of truth. Avienna sat in her room again, gazing at the second pig, the tin whistle clutched in her hands. Neatly, she placed a set of slender fingers over the holes and the top of the instrument in her mouth. Were there certain notes she had to play? Maybe one note tooted in repetition would do the trick. Blake didn't seem like he was playing a special tune whenever she heard him the first time.

She swore to herself. Why didn't he give her instructions before leaving? With a puff of air from her lips, Avienna blew into the whistle, timid at first, next time with more conviction. A shrill sound filled the room. Her fingers kept moving, changing up the notes. To her dismay, the pig stood on the base like the other one had, motionless, waiting.

Taking in a deep breath, she tried again. No luck. She threw the tin whistle on the bed. "Damn him!" Her fists clenched and she let out a string of silent obscenities in her head. Why was he making this so difficult? "He's playing me. That's what he's doing," Avienna murmured to herself. A thought hit her instantly, and her eyes lit up.

"Why didn't I think of this? I still have the first pig. That one will have to work. I saw it moving before he gave it to me." She scrambled to the drawer in her desk and pulled out the first pig. In the sunny afternoon glow peeping through the curtains of her bedroom, the golden surface flashed. Charming, seductive, tempting. With a few motions, Avienna turned the figuring in her hands, admiring the piece from different angles.

Clumsiness wasn't normally a flaw of hers, and why it happened, she'd never figure out. The pig slipped from her hands and came crashing down on the desk, hitting it with a hard, rude thud. Pieces scattered everywhere. The spindle dislodged from the base, sending the gold piglet flying across the room. Her mouth opened in horror. How would she ever explain this to Blake? Could he fix it? A flush filled her cheeks, and she sat on the bed, moping for a long while.

***

"Great day for a wedding." Devon elbowed Blake in the side.

"Couldn't ask for a prettier day." Blake stared at his friend dressed up in his wedding tuxedo. "If I were a girl, I'd marry you myself. You look pretty good." He nodded.

Devon let out a laugh. "I hate wearing these things. They choke the shit out of me."

"It'll only be this once. Or maybe on your wedding day."

"If I ever get that far." Devon tweaked at his bowtie, eyeing himself in the mirror.

Blake couldn't resist asking. "Have you asked that girl out, yet? The one at the bar?" He gazed at the grimace reflected in the mirror.

"I might do it the next time I see her, but she hasn't been back there lately."

"Hmm," said Blake, scratching his head. He didn't ask any more questions. Coincidence, busy schedule, or something else?"

The wedding planner came into Blake's room, "Knock, knock." She wore a big smile on her face. "Devon, you ready? Everyone else is getting into place."

Blake and Devon headed out the door. The girls and Abby had used a nearby hotel and drove over.

Chairs were placed next to the river. Abby and Eric would stand in front of the largest oak at the edge of the woods. A tent for the reception had been hoisted in the middle of a clear patch of land several yards from the cabin. Sometimes Blake laid out a blanket on clear starry nights and used the open area to gaze at the stars—and dream of Avienna.

A trio of string players sat playing wedding music. Ushers escorted guests to their particular sides, bride or groom. The minister stood in front of the oak tree waiting for the couple. In a few minutes, the bridal party would come out. Blake chose to stand farthest away from everyone, wanting to be both invited guest and surrogate wedding planner, helping the real planner make sure this event went off without a hitch.

The bridal party began their entrance to the ceremony site. Abby's mother started by being seated first. Blake knew when he met the lady where Abby got her sweet, wholesome good looks. It had been decided that the bridesmaids and groomsmen would walk together down the aisle. Just as Devon had told Blake the day he announced his participation, he and Cindy walked toward the minister, arm in arm.

Cindy didn't bother looking in Blake's direction, but kept her eyes straight ahead. When she turned briefly and viewed Devon, Blake noted how the two exchanged glances and smiled at each other. That action in and of itself wouldn't seem like anything out of the ordinary, but the way they looked at each other held something more. He sensed it and couldn't quite put his finger on the reason the gesture bore any more weight, other than two people being happily involved in their friends' special day.

The musicians stopped playing when the last of the party had taken their places. For a moment nothing was heard but the rush of the river. On cue, the players plucked and strummed their instruments. The traditional bridal march filtered through the air. The minister and musicians had microphones that sent their sounds through well-placed amplifiers.

Abby made her entrance, walking down the path of green toward the minister and Eric. Her dress of pure white trailed behind her, the veil covering a radiant face. A stylist had fashioned her hair in an elegant upsweep, topped by a glinting tiara. She held a bouquet of vibrant wildflowers in her hand. Blake held his breath. A quick pang of jealousy shot through him, dissipating the moment he saw someone out of the corner of his eye.

***

Avienna intended to give Blake a good scolding. He'd tricked her a second time, asking that she bare herself for those sweet, golden pigs. She'd loved every minute of it but wasn't about to let him know it right away. Regardless, she still wanted a working pig for her collection of curiosities. Today the traffic had slowed on Rapid Rivers Road, and she couldn't understand why.

The road usually flowed easily with cars, but today was different. When she neared Hoot Owl Hollow, the number of cars surrounding the place surprised her. What was going on? An insatiable curiosity set in. Avienna squeezed her car into a small space next to the shed where Blake kept his car parked. The sound of string instruments floating through the air mesmerized her as if she were under a magical spell.

Without any thought to her behavior or the appropriateness of it, she followed the sound, listening carefully. She kept walking away from the cabin, toward the river. When she spied the large reception tent, it all became clear. An event was going on, and it could only be one thing, by the type of music played.

"May I help you?" A pleasant woman walked up to her. "Are you one of the wedding guests?"

"Huh?" Avienna stood, stunned. She wracked her brain for the right answer. "Yes. Yes I am. I'm running late because I just got off work."

"That's all right, honey. If you move fast, you can catch everything before it gets under way." The lady pointed in the direction. "It's over there."

Avienna sprinted forward, more curious than ever. Was sneaky, sexy Blake getting married? Had she been duped, played for a fool? Anger washed all over her and tears stung her eyes. Every thought she could think of concerning Blake passed through her mind.

As she moved closer, she saw a figure in white completing her walk toward a minister. Avienna strained her eyes. Not thinking, she kept walking. The groom didn't look like Blake. What a relief, but when she saw who stood beside the groom, her heart nearly stopped. The man she wanted could have easily been the groom, if positions had been reversed.

She stared in shock. At that moment, Devon looked in her direction. He jerked his head up straighter and gazed back at her, nearly stepping out of line and walking her way. At that same moment, the minister stopped speaking, and the bridal couple turned and looked to see what had drawn Devon's attention.

Avienna blushed. All eyes turned in her direction, including the guests. Far off to the right, she finally detected Blake standing there looking at her. He moved immediately away from his position toward where she stood.

Filled with blinding embarrassment, Avienna took off running back toward the cabin. She hopped in her car, backed out of the tight space, praying she wouldn't hit anything, and peeled out onto Rapid Rivers Road. In the rearview mirror, she caught sight of Blake's reflection.

Chapter Eleven

Blake sat at his desk, scrolling on his laptop through auction and retail sites for the same penny whistle Aaron had given him. He needed another whistle to go with the pig. Of all the parts he'd ordered, whistles didn't make it on the list. Now his work was stranded without them. The brand had to be the same so the sound matched what was on the chips.

One more click and he found a website carrying what he needed. He clicked a button and ordered enough tin whistles to go with the rest of the pigs. A third pig he'd be working on, and still not one to show Lesander King. Time passed quickly, and only a couple of weeks remained before he needed to contact the person who would hopefully be his future boss. Blake liked to consider Mr. King more of a business partner than a boss.

It sounded better saying that over and over to himself. If he kept saying it, perhaps it would become true. He found working for himself put him in the driver's seat of his own destination. No one to tell him what to do or how to do it. No father to judge or from whom to win approval. The experience liberated him. Lesander King would be an idea supplier and marketer more than anything.

His cell phone rang. "Hello. Blake here."

"What the hell was she doing there?"

"Devon?" Blake sat up straighter in his chair. He immediately didn't like where this call was headed. "What's up, buddy?"

"Why did my girl from the bar show up unannounced at Abby's wedding? You know exactly what I'm talking about."

"Look, I don't know. I was as surprised as you were." That was the only truthful statement he might make during this whole conversation. Blake felt it in his bones.

"The whole thing makes no sense to me. There's absolutely no reason why she'd show up, at Abby's wedding of all places." Devon let out a huff.

Blake racked his brain for some kind of lame excuse, one that would get him off the phone. "Maybe it's a coincidence."

"That's the oddest coincidence I could ever imagine. It's just down and outright weird."

"Again, don't know, buddy. I tried to go after her and see what she wanted, what she was looking for, but she took off like a bat out of hell."

"Listen to me, Blake. The fact that she would stop at your place, park, get out of her car, and crash a wedding seems like more than just coincidence. She stopped for a reason."

"Don't you think the word 'crashing' is a bit overboard? That girl didn't crash anything. She turned tail and ran away as fast as she could." Blake blurted out, "Besides, weren't you happy to see her? I'm surprised you didn't split the scene and run after her yourself."

"I wanted to. Really bad, Blake. Man, she's hot."

"Yeah," said Blake, softly, "yeah, she is, Devon."

***

Avienna sat looking out the large picture window of her home. Working at the office with her father today instigated a splitting headache at the day's end. She sat holding a large glass of wine, hoping to calm her nerves. That wedding was beautiful. The whole scene hit her senses that day, and she still hadn't gotten over it.

"What are you thinking about?" Lesander King sat down next to his daughter, wine in hand.

"Not much. Resting more than anything." Avienna smiled at her father.

"You've seemed preoccupied for a while. Different. Something's bothering you." He took a sip of his wine, keeping an eye on Avienna.

She shook her head and returned her gaze toward the window. "I was out driving the other day, and I happened to see an outdoor wedding." Her father looked straight ahead and nodded, considering her words.

"And?" Lesander King replied.

"It was beautiful, from what I could tell just passing through." She wasn't about to tell him how she most likely made a fool of herself by showing up somewhere she didn't belong.

"Are you thinking about marriage a lot these days? It seems to be a topic that creeps up more frequently as of late. Or some round-about version of it." He smiled at his daughter.

"I guess I am." Avienna grimaced. "More than I care to admit." She sighed and took a drink from her glass.

"Sweetheart, that's something you'll have to work out totally on your own. I can help you out with a lot of things, but I don't think this is one of them. Marriage is a personal choice. You surely don't want your old man involved." He grinned and patted her on the leg.

Avienna watched as her father left for another part of the house. She stared out the window a long time. Her man had been there, standing next to the groom, looking handsome. But that man hadn't indicated that he truly wanted her. Sexy Blake had run after her. Good thing she ran faster or had a head start due to distance between them.

He owed her a working pig, but how would she ever explain the reason for showing up at a private ceremony unannounced? He'd ask her about it if they saw each other again. She knew that much. Forget about the pig and Devon and move on? Or make one last appeal to Blake that she wanted a dancing pig? What she wanted more than anything was her own wedding.

***

The cardboard box held the penny whistles Blake ordered several days ago. "Now to get this baby working and in the hands of Lesander King," he murmured to himself. The calendar showed only a week and a half left to go. Another little piglet had been attached to the spindle and placed into the base that held a sound chip. Blake picked up a whistle and started blowing.

Much to his relief, the pig whirled and lifted up on its two legs at the programmed time. This prototype was perfect. Nothing more to do with it, except package it up and call Mr. King. He reached for a small packing box he'd picked up at an office supply house.

"Not so fast."

Startled, Blake looked up.

Avienna's eyes flashed like a set of sapphires in the sun.

"What's up?" Blake asked, returning his attention to the pig.

"That's mine."

"Nope, this belongs to someone else. You have two of my pigs already. And the flute that makes them dance. One of them should be working, that much I know." He paused and wagged a finger at her.

Her cheeks colored. "Well, they don't. I tried out both of them."

"Look, said Blake, "I know the flute would work with the first one I gave you. It had the sound chip and everything in it."

"It didn't. I don't know why." Avienna scowled at him, hoping she sounded convincing enough.

"You're lying." Blake stopped and stared at her from across the counter. "You're not telling the truth, plain and simple. There is no good reason the first pig wouldn't dance, so tell me the real reason it didn't work."

"I dropped it, and it broke." The words barely came out of Avienna's mouth.

Blake stood there at the counter, stunned.

"Can I have another? I'll even bring the first two back, if that'll help." A pleading look washed over her face.

"Can you have another?" Blake mouthed the question in mock consideration. He turned his gaze and looked Avienna in the face. "You're mighty bold to ask. And to top it off, you've broken one. How do I know you won't break this one?"

"I'll be extra careful."

"If you want a third pig, you'll do more than be extra careful."

***

The cozy, charming bedroom had become a familiar place, lately. That's what Avienna thought as she lay naked on Blake's bed sheets, watching him undress. She liked the look of his body. Lean, sinewy, and most likely able to please her in more ways than one. He'd already proven it. A broken piglet commanded a high price, this time. She knew that much.

If doing whatever he wanted let her have a working pig and another round with him, she'd go through with it. Her gaze fell on the stiff cock, bobbing between his thighs.

Blake stood in front of her, the last of his clothing tossed haphazardly on the floor. His eyes glinted in the evening sun. A grin spread across his face. Avienna wanted to grasp the turgid cock standing tall and proud and watch him release while her finger toyed and played with him. Instead he walked over and crawled onto the bed, pushing her legs apart with his knees.

"I guess you know what's coming." He kissed her forehead, rubbing a finger lightly over the tattoo positioned over her right eyebrow. She closed her eyes. Blake focused his eyes, tracing around the curves of the large, ornate tattoo inked over the top part of her chest, awestruck at the exquisite work of the artist who had painstakingly used his needle to place and color every element in the drawing.

Her nipples stood erect, and Blake lowered his face and flicked out his tongue, teasing and suckling each of her breasts. Avienna let out a soft, satisfied moan. He sensed her thighs tightening on either side of him. She'd moved slightly beneath him, spreading herself wider. She surely ached like he did. His cock felt ready for action.

Blake reached for the sensitive bundle of nerves tucked hidden away at the top of her slit, and moved an eager, adept finger round and round. Avienna's eyes flew open, along with her blood red lips.

"You like that?" He whispered in her ear.

His fingers kept moving. She let out a whimper. Gently, he inserted two fingers deep inside her, smiling when he glided through a pool of wetness. Her body wanted him. Positioning himself, he aimed at her entrance and slid inside. Her flesh hugged his, firm yet willing. She'd relaxed, and he moved his hips back and forth, switching to circular motions when he craved a changed. He slipped in deeper with each thrust, her body yielding.

To his surprise, Aviennna reach up and toyed with his nipples, squeezing, rubbing, running her fingers over his sides and the front of his chest. When she grazed her long red nails over his skin, he let out a growl of pleasure. With a firm pair of hands, she reached around him and squeezed his buttocks, ending with a quick sharp pop on the smooth, muscular surface.

Blake took her in his arms and kissed her with every ounce of energy he had left. His tongue flirted with hers as he explored her mouth. He reached his tongue as far back as possible, running the tip over the walls of her mouth. She allowed him free reign. Each touch, rub, and gentle nip met with a look and sound of one in pure bliss.

When he'd tasted her lips and mouth long enough, he lowered his head and suckled her breasts another time, tonguing over and around her swollen nipples, ending with a gentle bite.

Avienna's inner muscles clenched and released Blake's cock buried inside her. He wanted this moment to last forever, wanted to remain locked in this embrace, feeling her hot flesh tug at his.

His balls ached, a delicious gnawing pain he wanted to keep and end at the same time. He rubbed harder against her, strategically moving over her clit. She let out a small shout and bucked under him. Blake smiled, feeling the internal spasms contract and release around his cock. When she finished, he couldn't hold on anymore, but let go, emptying himself completely.

The two lay still on the bed, nothing, no sound but their heavy breathing. Blake ran his finger over her hair, feeling the silkiness of her golden locks. In the afterglow of passionate love-making, Avienna was the most beautiful creature he'd ever seen, ever held in his arms. She belonged to him, whether she knew it or not. He knew it, and that was what mattered most.

He lifted himself up a little. Avienna threw her arms around her head, cradling it with her hands. Blake blinked several times, focusing on a peculiar image on the inside of the upper aspect of her left arm. This image had escaped him the first time, or she did a good job of hiding it when he'd first suckled those luscious breasts.

"What the hell?" He rubbed his finger over a small tattoo, the size of a silver half dollar. It had been infused with colors that made the image looked like it glowed pure gold. A circle with a crown on the inside. Above the image, the word "Princess".

Avienna turned her head in the direction where his fingers caressed her skin. She looked back at him and smiled.

"What is this? What does it mean?" Blake's heart pounded. Why would she have a tattoo drawn in this design? The prospective answer filled him with a certain dread.

"It's a family business logo. My father is a business man, and I work with him. He calls me his little princess." She laughed. "You know how dads are."

Blake swallowed hard. "I hear that. Don't have sisters, but I know my dad would have watched them like a hawk."

The last thing he needed to be doing was getting it on hot and heavy with Lesander King's daughter. He played it cool, getting up from the bed and quickly dressing. Avienna did the same. She left Blake's cabin with her golden piglet and the flute. He watched her drive off. This time there was nothing to bring her back. He spent the remainder of the evening at home, sipping wine, and mourning his loss.

***

The shrill tinkling of his cell phone stopped work on the new piglet Blake had placed in his trusty vice.

"This is Blake."

"Mr. McCallahan?" The voice belonged to a female he didn't recognize.

"Yes."

"I'm calling from Lesander King's office.

"Okay." Blake placed the drill on the table. He still had some time left to get a pig ready. Why was he receiving a call?

"Mr. King wants to see you right now, if you can possibly get away. He wants the item he gave you. Says he needs it back immediately."

"Oh?" Blake winced. This couldn't possibly be happening. "Did he say why? I still have a few days left."

"From what I gather, he feels like you've had enough time to complete the project he gave you. Unless there's a reason you can't come to the office now, he's insisting on meeting with you."

"Sure, I can do that. I'll be on my way."

"Thank you, Mr. McCallahan. He will be happy to hear that. Good-bye."

Click. The line disconnected.

"Damn!" Blake scratched his head and looked around his work room. "This sucks." He had to get someone to watch the shop while he made this ill-timed meeting with Lesander King. Cindy would have come in handy right now, but he'd blown that offer the night he ended it all with her.

"Hey, Blake?" A voice came across the room from the front door.

"Yeah. How's it going?"

One of his artisan instructors stood in front of him.

"Just wanted to let you know I was filling in this week. You need anything?"

"Do you know of anyone who can hightail it over here and run my shop? I've been called in for an urgent meeting with someone."

The man raised his eyebrows. "Oh? I think I can get one of my friends to do it. She's retired, but has lots of retail experience."

"Call and get her over here. I'll even pay extra for such a short notice."

Blake looked down at the pig. Could he possibly get one ready? He shook his head. Though he'd gotten better with each piece, it took time to place everything in working order. With a heavy feeling growing in the pit of his stomach, he gathered up the box with the remaining pigs, including the one removed from his vice. The drive to King's office couldn't end quickly enough.

***

Inside the waiting room, Blake sat, rehearsing excuses he could give Mr. King for why he hadn't produced something creative with the golden pigs after all this time.

"Mr. King will see you now." Another different woman sat behind the reception desk.

He acknowledged hearing the statement and gathered up the box. Any prospects of landing a position on King's team had vanished, unless he could appeal in some manner. But how?

"Good to see you again, Mr. McCallahan." Lesander King stepped out from behind the desk, extending a hand. Blake shook it. "Do you have something wonderful to show me?" King motioned for Blake to follow him to the room where they had first discussed the pigs. The two men sat at the table.

"Mr. King, I have to confess that I don't have a prototype ready to show you today, but I do have a working idea of what to do with the pigs."

"Oh?" The man's eyebrows furrowed. "After all this time, you don't have a finished product, even a rough presentation of one? Why?"

Blake adjusted his collar and cleared his throat. "I've been working hard on this project. And my idea works well. It's just that some personal things came up unexpected, and it's set me back a little."

King frowned. "I'm sorry to hear that some hardships set you back, but giving me a call much earlier would have settled everything better in my mind." He sat back, scrutinizing Blake. "But coming here at the last minute, telling me you don't have anything is simply unacceptable."

"Sir, not meaning any disrespect, I still had a few days left. That would have given me a little more time."

"No disrespect taken, Mr. McCallahan, but now it sounds like you're pinning this on me, that I called you too early, or something like that." The older man forced a fake smile. "I'll take the box of pigs and find another person who might be able to come up with something. Actually the gentleman I'm thinking of says he's created several interesting projects that he sells at an artisan store on the main strip here in Gatlinburg.

Blake's eyes widened. King either referred to Devon or possibly Aaron, but Devon seemed the most likely. He'd mentioned interviewing with King. "Sir, would you reconsider and give me another couple of days? I'll have something ready for you."

"No, I won't give you another couple of days. You've had weeks to do this." King reached out and opened the box. "There are three pigs missing. What did you do with them?"

"Sir, some of them became damaged. I had to practice making the prototypes."

"And you simply didn't put them back in the box as is? That would have been much more acceptable than coming in here with three pigs gone." He stood up, scowling. "I think we're finished here, Mr. McCallahan. I had high hopes for you, but this arrangement isn't going to work between us." King pointed toward the door. "You know the way out."

Numb with disappointment, Blake silently left the room, headed back down the hallway and out of the building. He needed other ways to expand his business. His income barely paid the bills and gave him a measly salary, nothing remotely near his father's earnings nor Lesander King's. The mysterious golden box his dad gave him might as well be out of reach. He only had several weeks to go before that opportunity became as lost as King's project.

***

"What do you want to do for a celebration, Dad?" Avienna sat across from her father's desk.

Lesander King leaned back in his fine black leather chair and gazed at his daughter. "Don't know. Any grand ideas?" He smiled.

"I think a celebration event would be a nice way to welcome your new designers."

"A catered affair at one of the hotels, or something here at the office?"

Avienna thought for a moment, tapping a pen against her clipboard. "How about The Grand View Hotel on top of the hill here in Gatlinburg?"

The older gentleman sat up straight. "Not a bad idea. Any special program we could add, some entertainment, prizes?"

"Your designers are men, aren't they?"

"I have one female, but the other four are men." He squinted at his daughter. "Why would it matter about them being men or women?"

"Because I have an idea that will really be crazy, but it's something I'm wanting to do."

"What's that?"

"I want to hold a contest, and I will be the prize."

Lesander King's face showed no emotion, his eyes nearly glazing over like someone in the throes of death. "Come again," he said, finding his voice.

"I want a husband, and I'm thinking that anyone you hired would meet your approval."

"And just how do you equate a job position with being a superb husband to my one and only beloved daughter? Have you gone insane?"

"No, I haven't gone insane." Avienna grimaced.

"What's wrong with dating, like normal people?" King's voice rose in pitch.

"This way will be faster. Besides, my internal clock's ticking."

"Good, Lord. Avienna, you can't be serious." He scowled at his daughter. "No, I simply can't allow this sort of folly. I don't care how desperate you are. It's a foolhardy thing to do."

"I could do it without your permission, but I'd have to think a little harder on the details. At least with males already in one place, at a celebration event, it couldn't hurt to try." She smiled back at her father.

"Avienna, I love you. I think you're the most beautiful girl in the world. But as much as I have a father's love that runs deep, knows no bounds, other men may not feel exactly the same way. Know what I mean?"

"I know, but somehow I think my true love will be found in one of your designers. It will look like an arranged marriage, only not." Avienna's gaze met her dad's. "Other countries have been doing similar things like this since the beginning of time. Works for them." She grinned.

King threw up his hands in exasperation. "You don't know that. We never talk to people who've done it."

"Let's do it. Are you with me?"

"I guess so, if that's what you want more than anything."

"I do."

***

Aaron Trolle sat with his steaming mug of coffee in front of his lips. He and Blake sat on the front porch of the cabin at Hoot Owl Hollow. "I hear King is throwing a big shindig at the Grand View Hotel for his new hires. You looking forward to it?" He looked over at Blake. "Came over to congratulate you. I never heard if he liked your idea or not."

Blake stared down at his cup, watching the wispy clouds of steam rise from the surface. "About that."

Aaron bolted upright in his rocker. "What do you mean?"

"Trust me, Professor Trolle, you won't be happy when I tell you. I wasn't able to get the project out to him like I had planned. He called me a little too soon."

"Too soon?" Aaron's words ended on a high note. "C'mon, Blake. You had weeks to do this thing. Get it all done and out the door onto his desk. What on earth happened?" The man's face clouded with irritation.

"I don't really know how to answer that, honestly." Blake found the courage to look in the direction of his former professor. Other than Calin Shepherd, he had been the biggest helper since his arrival from Johnson City.

Aaron continued his rant. "You don't know how to answer that. What was so earth-shattering and time-consuming that you couldn't get his project completed in a timely manner? You created bigger projects in a shorter amount of time when you were at Calin's. Is there something in the mountain air that finally got the better of you?"

"Look, I'm going to start coming up with some other project ideas. I've had some on the back burner. All I'll need to do is flesh them out a little."

"Lesander King has a ready market for a lot of things. Would have saved you a world of time." Aaron shook his head in disgust. "I can't believe after all this, you've blown it."

Blake said nothing.

The men finished their coffee in silence. Aaron got up to leave.

"The event is this weekend at 6 pm. I'm heartbroken that you won't be part of it."

Blake sat in thought, watching the sun dip below the horizon. He also thought about Avienna and the golden tattoo on her arm. No doubt about it, she was Lesander King's daughter. He would go to the so-called shindig and crash that party, whether King liked it or not. Avienna would be there. She had a pig that worked, and her father needed to know about it.

Chapter Twelve

A large meeting room inside the Grand View Hotel buzzed with people, office staff from Lesander King's business, the newly hired designers, along with corporate contacts and clients. Along a wall at the opposite side of the room stood a steaming buffet holding a delectable choice of steak, chicken medallions, fish, three cuts of vegetables, bread, and a section with salad items, including dressing. A dessert bar finished off the presentation.

Along another wall, two bartenders mixed drinks and poured wine with expert speed. Uniformed ladies wound through the crowd, jotting drink orders, delivering food, and removing soiled plates from tables. A small band played in one corner. People mingled, chatting, smiling, comparing business information. The designers stayed together in one small group, each one sharing how they won a slot in the most coveted of positions.

Blake parked his car in the gargantuan parking lot and made his way to the hotel entrance. He had dressed in a handsome casual ensemble so he wouldn't appear out of place. Thoughts of seeing Avienna sent his heart racing. His stomach clenched as a wave of the jitters set in. He'd see Lesander King, and he already prepared himself for getting the old heave-ho if King decided to pitch him out of the hotel.

He had to see Avienna and talk her into showing Lesander King the dancing golden pig. It was a last-ditch effort to restore a piece of his life that had listed to one side and was nearly sinking. When he reached the lobby, a large sign on an easel announced the King Reception and the number of the meeting room for the event.

Blake sucked in his breath and headed in the right direction. Loud music and the sound of a jolly crowd met his hears the moment he rounded the hall. Plucking up his last ounce of courage, he opened the door and stepped inside.

Devon saw him right away and rushed over. "You're late. What held you up?"

"Sorry, man. Had things to take care of." Blake looked around and smiled at Devon. "Great party."

"Go get some food. It's great. Drinks are good too." Devon winked and patted Blake on the shoulder.

Blake nodded and smiled at the chosen designers standing with Devon and carefully stepped toward the buffet. He really shouldn't be doing this. It was wrong, plain and simple. He hung back, watching everyone. No matter what his friend suggested, he was not helping himself to a buffet and drinks. His eyes wandered over groups of people talking, and that's when he spied Avienna.

She looked more beautiful than ever, wearing a silver sparkly tight-fitting dress, ending right above the knees. Her hair had been styled in her trademark upsweep, but this time, a small arrangement of flowers sat in place of the one lone flower she normally wore. A few strings of sparkling tiny crystal beads dripped down the side of her hair. Showcased under the glow of the ceiling lights, her red lips glistened.

Lust grew inside Blake. He wanted her more than ever right now. If he had his way about it, he'd whisk her away to a private hotel room inside this gorgeous building. There he would have her to himself and take her over and over again. He'd order room service, and they would indulge in the pleasure of each other for another round.

"Can I get something for you, sir?"

Blake jumped at the voice. "Hmm? Oh, nothing for me right now." He shook his head at the server who stood in front of him. She nodded and walked to the next person a few feet away.

"You not hungry?" Devon came up to Blake and stood beside him.

"I don't think so. I grabbed a bite before I came."

"Why would you do that when you knew we were coming here?"

"Don't know." Blake stared back at Devon. "It's okay, mom. I won't starve."

"Cut it out. You seem nervous for some reason. What's wrong with you?"

"Nothing. Why would you say that?" Blake frowned.

"You're not speaking to anyone. You're not eating like everyone." Devon mumbled in Blake's ear. "It's like you don't belong here. That's how you're acting."

"Drop it, Devon. I've just about had it with the questions."

Devon shook his head. "That's exactly what I'm talking about, man."

The thought hit Blake hard. He had to ask. "Why didn't you bring Cindy as your date? You two seemed pretty cozy at Abby's wedding."

"We weren't cozy. You don't know what you're talking about. She's a nice girl, but we're not anything more than good friends."

"How good?" Blake grinned.

"You're a nosy ass, Blake. I swear . . ."

"What are you holding out for?"

"That one over there." Devon pointed in Avienna's direction. "I'm going to ask her out tonight, when I can get her away from people."

Blake flushed. Someday this had to end. The quicker the better. Better still if he could reach Avienna before his buddy Devon.

"Excuse me. May I have everyone's attention?" Lesander King stood at the front of the room, tapping a spoon against a water glass. Everyone stopped speaking and turned their attention in his direction.

Blake stiffened and looked toward the man who could have been his ticket to a better future. Devon stood still beside his friend. Both exchanged quick questioning glances when Avienna quickly excused herself from a circle of listeners and rushed to her father's side.

Lesander King spoke, "I first want to thank everyone for joining us tonight. We want to honor our new designers who have joined our team. I've hand-picked the best of the best, and I'm proud of all of them."

Everyone in the room broke into a round of applause.

"But there is one special person in my life that will always be my pride and joy, and that's my beautiful daughter, Avienna." He side-hugged his daughter. Another round of applause rippled through the room. "She helps this business more than anyone knows, always working in the background, making sure everything is in tip top shape. I couldn't do it without her." Avienna smiled at the audience.

King continued, "I usually take Avienna's advice on things because I trust her. She knows my business, what I like, what I'm looking for. But one day, she asked me a question that still has me stumped." He looked at his daughter and displayed a wry smile. "She finally confessed to me that she wants a partner in life, someone to share all her joys and heartaches, wants a family of her own." Everyone clapped.

"That may not sound unusual," said Lesander King. "All us married folks have been at that same place before we ended up with the wonderful spouses we have right now. Here's the interesting part that she has proposed to me, and I'm proposing it now to you."

The room grew still, not a tinkle from an ice cube in a glass, not sound from the guests. Avienna stared out into the room, still with a sober look on her face.

"Avienna wants a husband, and she wants him tonight."

Everyone gasped. Blake and Devon stared wide-eyed at each other.

"Now's my chance," Devon whispered to Blake.

Blake merely smiled and said nothing. The only one who would end up as Avienna's husband would be him. He'd see to that.

"What does a man have to do to earn that privilege, good sir?" Devon unabashedly called out to Mr. King.

Blake wanted to duck and run.

"I'm glad you asked," said King. "C'mon up here, son. Don't be shy. Come on up." The gentleman motioned for Devon to come forward. Avienna's cheeks flushed. Blake's heart sank.

"I have to tell you," continued King, "I'm extremely proud of you. You're going to be one of my top people. I can tell." He looked toward the group of remaining designers standing and staring at each other with questioning looks on their faces. "But I have great confidence in my other designers too. You'll have some stiff competition." He laughed, patting Devon on the back while keeping his gaze on the small group.

"I'm going to answer your question. Avienna set up the rules. I tried to talk her out of it, but she made me promise. So here it is. Any interested male will step up here with us and answer a question. The winner wins her."

The room quietened. Guests glanced at each other. Many men stepped back. The married men looked at their wives, smiled, and shook their heads.

"Who's interested?" Lesander King looked at Devon. "You staying or going?"

"I'm in, sir. Wouldn't miss this opportunity for the world."

Avienna winked at Devon and turned her gaze back to the audience. No one moved toward the front. Blake looked around. He grinned. This was a sign of destiny. He pushed his way through the crowd and stood in front of Lesander King. Avienna's face turned a bright pink.

"I'd like to throw my hat in the ring, sir, if I may." Blake looked straight into Lesander King's eyes.

The man frowned, holding the microphone away from his mouth. He leaned over and whispered, "Just what the hell are you doing here?"

"I heard about the party from Aaron Trolle," Blake whispered back. "You owe me a fair chance at this."

"I don't owe you a damn thing. You failed me."

Devon watched with amusement. Avienna's face wore a look of concern.

"Sir, I have a project for you. I promise I do, and I think you'll like it." Blake turned and looked at the guests and back to King. "We can either settle it here out in the open, or you can let me participate and not say a word."

"I can have you thrown out of here. That's what I can do." Lesander King glanced up and looked out toward the back of the room.

"Please let me participate, and I won't bother you again for anything else." Blake placed his hand on King's arm. "Please, as a man of honor."

"Dad, let him." Avienna had stepped over and gently pushed her dad back. "It's okay. It's not like people are rushing up here."

"I warned you about that." King scowled.

"Let this man participate," said Avienna. Her words came out more emphatic this time. "It's my life. I'll take the consequences."

The gentleman straightened up, gazed out at his guest, and spoke into the microphone, "It seems as if we have another contender. Anyone else want to join these two men? Anyone?"

No one came forward.

"Very well, then. We'll start." King forced a smile and asked the first question, "What is the meaning of Avienna's tattoo?" He pointed to the markings below her neck line.

The guests murmured, looking around at each other with surprised expressions. Devon appeared stumped. He looked quickly at Blake, who merely stood with an air of smugness on his face.

Devon thought a few seconds and replied, shrugging, "She likes the wings. The image reminds her of being lifted up so she can soar to heights of happiness."

Avienna wagged her head back and forth lightly, considering his words. She and her father exchanged glances. She shook her head. Mr. King scowled and angled his head toward Blake.

Blake cleared his throat. "She wears the butterfly because it reminds her that she has freedom to do whatever she wants, and nothing can hold her down."

Lesander King narrowed his eyes, irritated. Avienna told her father, "He's right about that. I've told you the same thing."

The room broke out in a chorus of murmurs. Women whispered to each other. Men stood surprised, watching the contest in front of them.

"Yes, you have, dear," the man answered through gritted teeth. He forced a smile at his guests and held up a hand. "But let's not end here. I have a question I want to ask." King looked at his daughter. "Would you let me ask?"

"Of course," she said, smiling.

"What else does Avienna have in the way of a tattoo? This one is quite special. Where is it located, and what does it mean?"

Devon once again wore a helpless look on his face. He looked at Blake for answers, a hint.

Blake stood staring at Avienna and said nothing.

"Um, well . . . there is the tattoo above her right eye. It's an ancient symbol for wealth and prosperity." He grinned at King and Avienna. Aviena's face had grown solemn. Blake's confidence soared.

"Not correct, I'm afraid," answered King. "Your turn." He faced Blake with a nearly defeated look on his face.

Blake smiled. He spoke clearly into the microphone. "On the inside of the upper portion of her left arm, there is a bright, golden tattoo of the family business logo. It's a crown inside a circle with the word 'Princess' above it."

Lesander King's face turned red; his eyes blazed. Devon's face blanched with defeat. Avienna stood speechless, suddenly interested in staring at the floor.

"That's correct," said Mr. King, "but we're not done. Not just yet."

Avienna's eyes shot wide open. She turned and stared at her father.

"Tell you what, princess, since you want a husband, why not go all the way?"

The guests gasped.

"Oh, not like that," said the gentleman. "Where are your minds?" He grinned. I'll not be happy until there's one more thing to do."

"What's that?" Avienna asked. Her voice cracked out barely above a whisper.

"Since you seem to harbor a daring streak, I figure you must get it from me." King glanced at his daughter. "I want you two men to sleep with my daughter. In the same bed. Whomever she is facing when I check the room in the morning will be her husband."

Lesander King looked at the guests and again at his daughter, Devon, and Blake. "I'll get a room with a king-size bed. That will hold the three of you." He pulled back a sleeve and studied his watch. "We'll start this last contest at midnight. At 8 a.m. I'll check on everyone."

"Sounds good to me," Blake said.

"I guess so." Devon didn't look quite convinced.

"Should be interesting." Avienna glanced over at her father. "You know how to push the limits, don't you?"

"I didn't make it in this business, my dear, by being a gutless pushover. Sometimes you gotta give it all you got." King turned his attention back on his guests. "Eat, drink, and be merry, my friends. For this is a pre-celebration of my daughter's future wedding."

Everyone clapped.

Blake didn't speak to Devon or Avienna but walked toward the humble group of new designers and struck up a new conversation. Out of the corner of his eye, Blake watched Devon eating more food and drinking. It was like the night at the bar months ago, when they first saw Avienna, and he had to drive his friend home because of his stumbling-blind drunken state.

Somewhere in Blake's gut, he knew he could turn this situation to his advantage. His stomach rumbled, but no matter how hungry he was, he would not over-indulge in food and drink. Not here at Lesander King's party. He'd already pushed the envelope. Excusing himself from the group, he slipped out into the lobby.

The gift shop would close in ten minutes. Blake headed inside and looked around. Perfect. He spied a bag of dried fruit, which he picked up, along with a chocolate bar filled with caramel and nuts. These would be dinner once he and his competition and future wife turned in at midnight. That was what Avienna would be soon. His wife.

He slipped the candy bar and bag of dried fruit in his pocket and returned to the party. The food buffet had closed down, but alcohol flowed unchecked. Devon sucked down more than his fair share. Blake watched on, not saying a word. No one was driving anywhere tonight, and the three of them would be parking themselves in a hotel room.

When the party ended, Lesander King led the way to a room he'd reserved for the last stint of the contest. Inserting the key card, he twisted the handle and opened the door. Refreshing cool air hit Blake's face. He let out a sigh. His stomach ached from hunger. When that door closed, he'd dive into the bag of dried fruit.

"Okay, everyone, once I'm gone, no one leaves this room until I come in at 8 a.m. tomorrow morning. I'm having a couple of my staff sit outside the room to make sure nothing happens. Understood?" Blake, Devon, and Avienna nodded.

"I guess we sleep in our clothes?" Devon asked. He held out his hands to steady himself.

The walk from the party area to the room had been a wobbly one. Blake had hung back, allowing King and Avienna to walk ahead while he kept an eye on Devon.

Lesander King exchanged glances with each one. "Looks that way. Or you can sleep in the buff. Don't care. Not my problem. All of you agreed to this crazy stunt. I'm just here to oblige." He turned to his daughter. "I hope you find this whole ordeal worth it."

"It'll be worth it." She lifted her chin up, determined.

"Good-night." The older gentleman left the room, and the door shut behind him with a resounding dull thud.

"I guess that's that." Blake narrowed his eyes. "Avienna, it's a no-brainer for you. You'll be in the middle. Devon, which side do you want?"

"The one closest to . . ." Devon held out a wavering finger toward the bathroom.

"Yeah, I have a feeling that's a good choice, buddy."

Avienna walked over to Devon. "Do you want to loosen your shirt? Get more comfortable? Maybe I can bring you a cold cloth."

She walked briskly to the bathroom and came back with a damp cloth. Blake watched with half-amusement as Avienna tended to Devon, wiping down his face, smoothing his hair. The sight of it all irritated him. Did Avienna enjoy any of the time they spent together in his bedroom?

Why did she still care about Devon, the man who didn't even get up the nerve to ask her out on an honest date? The man who only went after her tonight because, in his arrogance, he thought he'd actually win her over.

"Don't know about you two, but I'm turning in. I'm exhausted." Blake headed toward the side of the bed next to the nightstand, took off his shoes and jacket, and stretched out on the bed. He placed his snacks next to him and closed his eyes. Never mind the fact Avienna kept her attention on Devon, ignoring him completely when he announced he was going to bed.

About one-thirty, Blake awoke. His stomach still ached. Devon had been restless, drifting in and out of sleep, but that hadn't deterred Avienna, who remained curled next to him, steadfast, with her head nestled against his chest. She faced him. That alone disturbed Blake. Did she ever change positions during the night, or was she a sleeper who stayed locked in one place?

The lights from the parking lot below brightened up the room enough to keep it free from total darkness. Blake sat up, rubbed his eyes, and quietly headed to the bathroom, where he urinated in the toilet. He avoided looking in Avienna's direction when he returned to bed. He knew she had lifted her head and watched intently the first moment he got up.

His belly rumbled. One twist of the wrapper, and a bite of the chocolate bar played a sweet harmony of flavors on his tongue. The second bite was better than the first. On impulse he hopped back off the bed and made himself a cup of coffee from the mini coffee maker.

He sat in one of the arm chairs by the window, munching on the sweet confection and sipping coffee. When he finished his first cup, he made another and grabbed his bag of dried fruit. The vision of Avienna's intent eyes in his direction fired him up. No matter how long she stared at him, he wouldn't acknowledge her. She could watch him all night, for all he cared.

The ugly truth: he did care. Cared so much it hurt. Short of forcing her to look at him until morning, there was nothing else he could do. He reclined his head back and closed his eyes. The sound of Devon moving around woke him up.

Blake sat up with a start. His gaze landed on Avienna perched on the end of the bed, her back turned away from him. An awful sound of retching came from the bathroom. For a moment he struggled against his own sudden urge to vomit. Devon gagged again and let out another round of sickness.

Avienna clutched at the sheets, watching the bathroom door. Blake shook his head in disgust. If she wanted a man who couldn't contain his liquor along with not being able to make a decision on whether or not to ask a woman out, Devon was her man. She turned and looked in Blake's direction. He answered by popping some more dried fruit in his mouth. Nothing better than the taste of raisins, cranberry, and kiwi at . . . he glanced at the clock. Two-thirty in the morning.

This was going to be a long night, and how it would end was anybody's guess. Devon stumbled back into bed, nearly tripping over Avienna. She let out a sharp cry and rubbed her leg. Blake swallowed down a few more pieces of fruit. Tired of sitting in the uncomfortable armchair, he returned to bed. Did Devon rinse his mouth out at all? An undeniable sour odor permeated the air.

Come to think of it, he didn't remember his friend turning on the sink. Worse, he didn't recall hearing the toilet flush, either. The rancid smell grew stronger, and Blake sincerely wished for another cup of fresh-brewed coffee to kill the odor. Lifting up the bag of fruit, he lowered his face over the top, inhaling the sweet aroma of sugar.

Blake popped a few more pieces in his mouth. The taste diminished the foul air filling his nose. Avienna stirred beside him. The trailing of her fingernail over his arm startled him, and he nearly strangled on a kiwi slice. Still, he refused to acknowledge her.

"What you got?" Avienna whispered.

"Nothing."

She lifted her head. "Yes, you do. I want some."

"You ate. I didn't." Blake sucked on a cranberry.

"Why not?"

"I crashed your dad's fancy party. I couldn't snarf his food down. He nearly kicked my ass as it was."

"No, he didn't."

She trailed her finger down his arm again.

If she didn't stop coming on to him, Blake would throw the bag of fruit across the room, take her in his arms, and smother her with kisses. Dried cranberries tasted mighty sweet, but nothing would compare to the unadulterated sweetness of sucking on one of Avienna's nipples.

His cock stiffened at the thought. All of him stiffened when Avienna cleverly smoothed her arm down his thigh and landed a hand on the hardened bulge between his legs.

"Stop that," whispered Blake.

"I want a bite."

"Then will you stop?"

"Maybe."

Blake caught a hint of her smile in the shadowy light of the room. He reached in and pulled out a kiwi slice. "You want this?"

She sat up, her smile wider. He pulled the fruit away, teasing. Her hand clamped down on him. Blake let out a loud grunt. Devon mumbled in his sleep.

"Shh, no teasing," whispered Avienna in earnest.

"This is all you get." Blake held the fruit to her mouth, watching with interest as Avienna took the piece between her teeth and ate.

"Just one more?"

"Not gonna happen. Again, you ate. I didn't." Blake tipped the bag, poured the few remaining raisins and cranberries in his mouth, and chewed. "Mmm, that was good." He laid his head on the pillow. The empty bag went sailing through the air and onto the floor. Avienna lay in his direction, staring at him.

"What?"

"I can't believe you didn't give me another bite. That was mean."

"Sorry, a man's gotta do what a man's gotta do." Blake chuckled to himself. He had her full attention.

"He stinks. You smell good," she said whispering in his ear.

Blake flipped over so the two faced each other, nose to nose. "I try."

She giggled and snuggled her face against his chest. He wrapped his arms around her and held her close. If they could stay locked down like this, holding each other until Lesander King woke them up, he would have the love of his life forever. Blake closed his eyes and dreamed of Avienna and the golden box.

Chapter Thirteen

"Looks like you made your choice." Lesander King stood at the foot of the bed, frowning.

Blake squinted through sleepy eyes at the older gentleman. Avienna stirred awake, turning her face away from Blake's chest. She sat up and stared at her father.

All three turned in Devon's direction, noting the younger man propped against his pillow. An ashen face held grim sadness, giving him a look of someone who had lost their best friend.

"You look pretty rough, young man," said Lesander King, moving to Devon's side of the bed.

"He had a bad night, dad. Don't ask." Avienna turned to Devon, patting him on the thigh. "You had lots of chances to ask me out. I hinted more than once that I was interested. What happened?"

Devon shook his head. "Don't know. Wanted to play it nice and slow, I guess?"

"Sometimes you gotta make a more decisive move before an opportunity slips away. You lose out muddling things around in your head too much." The older gentleman gazed at Devon, sadness brewing in his eyes. "And that's what happened here."

"Hello, anybody give a damn about me?" Blake sat up on the side of the bed, irritation firing him wide awake.

Both Avienna and Lesander King focused their attention back on Blake.

"You know what," he said, glaring at the perplexed girl beside him, "we can call this whole thing off. If you have the hots for him that bad, then have at it. I simply don't care anymore." Blake got up, slipped on his shoes and grabbed his jacket. "We had a lark doing this fascinating contest, but in the end, we're back to reality."

Lesander King said nothing, staring open-mouthed at Blake.

"As for you, sir, thank you for entertaining such an insane contest. Shows you have a sense of humor." Blake brushed passed the older man. "Oh, if you're really interested in the project I made for you, just ask your dear daughter. She knows all about it."

Avienna and her father watched in stunned silence as Blake left the room.

Devon tapped Avienna's shoulder. "I think he's serious about what he said. Do you think there would be a chance between us? If you really want it, that is." A corner of his mouth pulled into a lopsided grin.

Avienna didn't say anything. She slipped on her shoes and left the two men in the hotel room.

***

Blake pulled into his parking shed, cut off the engine, and rested his head back on the car seat. "Damn!" He hit the steering wheel in anger. "I knew it was too good to be true." His heart hurt. Would the dreary mood overwhelming him right now ever go away? The whole ordeal had been a missed opportunity. For him. What made him think he could win her over? He got out of the car and headed to the river.

Sitting on a large, smooth rock, he gazed out over the currents, listening to the swirl of the water rushing by. The river always soothed him, but today it didn't readily do the trick. He'd find another girl. A rational mind told him so. Blake didn't want another girl. He wanted only one, and the only one wanted another. None of it made sense.

Why had Avienna agreed to their sexy interludes? Wanting a golden pig and doing anything for it seemed a bit overboard. He refused to think of her as merely a loose woman who engaged in wild, wiley moments for sheer thrills. People could fool you.

Maybe she had truly fooled him, and he fell for it. Blake looked behind him. This site had been the place for Abby's wedding not long ago. It should be the same place for his now.

He hugged his knees, resting his head on top. The water would wash his hurt downstream, carry it far away if he looked at it long enough. Tomorrow, he'd start fresh and new. On the final day that should be his wedding day, he'd make a trip back to Johnson City, hand the golden box back to Jared, and explain why he couldn't fulfill a promise he'd made years ago.

"Hey, stranger."

Blake tensed. He turned and viewed Avienna picking her way over the stones to where he sat. She settled down beside him, tucking both knees close to her body. He didn't say anything but looked away, trying his best to ignore her. They both sat, neither saying anything. No matter how hard the effort, he couldn't act like she wasn't beside him. Did he want her gone for good this time? All he'd have to do is tell her to go.

"Are we going to sit here all day and not talk?"

He glanced at her and back to the water. Part of him wanted to scream, asking why she bothered coming over at all. Her continued preference for Devon hurt, bit him to the core. No way of denying the fact any longer.

"Why are you here?" he said in a controlled voice.

"I wasn't about to let you walk out without saying anything. I didn't like how it all went down."

"I let you off the hook. Go back to Devon."

Avienna sat in silence a moment, considering an answer. "You won fair and square. Devon lost the same way."

"Did you hear what I just said?" Blake sensed his voice getting louder.

She licked her lips and kept her eyes focused on the river. After another round of silence, Avienna spoke again, "I came here because I wanted to. Devon made an offer after you left. I won't lie about that. I didn't take him up on it."

Blake glared at her. "What do you want, then?"

"I want you to make good on the promise." She turned her face toward him.

"What promise? There is no promise. It was a silly game."

"Why did you agree to it?"

"Why did you agree to it?" Blake gestured with his hand. "All of it. Letting me have my way with you. Why?"

"Because I wanted to." Avienna blinked several times, keeping her eyes on Blake.

"Let's just get to the point. You want another man. I honestly don't think I can live with knowing that I'll always be second fiddle." He let out a mock chuckle. "Call me selfish, but I like being number one."

"If you ask me, neither you nor Devon seemed to care about being my number one."

"What the hell? Why would you say that?" Blake clenched his fists, frustrated.

"You didn't pursue me, either. Not really." Avienna's gaze burned with an intensity that prodded Blake to think long and hard about what she said. "Tell me, what would you have done had I never come into your shop? More than that, what would you have done if I never came back after the first time—or the second?"

Blake swallowed hard. She had him, her questions gripping around his virtual neck so tight he nearly choked. What would he have done?

"As I see it," Avienna continued, "neither of you seemed all that interested. I had different hopes for you, especially after what we did. That's why I came back—and for the pigs—they are cute. Won't lie about that, either. Again, you never asked me out on a formal date, never pursued. I had to be the one coming back. And here I am again." She looked away, fidgeting with her fingers.

"There's one thing you need to know," answered Blake. "I rigged those pigs and left out the flute, hoping you would come back when they didn't work."

Avienna shook her head. "Playing games is fun with the right person at the right time, but in the end a girl wants to know she's more than a game."

Blake stared down in shame. He'd broken Cindy's heart, and now Avienna's words slapped his soul. "The last thing I'd ever want to do is hurt you."

"What's wrong with you? With Devon? What is it with men?"

"I don't know." Blake shook his head. "If I knew the answer, I could make a fortune."

Avienna moved to get up, Blake, grabbed her hand. "Don't go. Sit down." He scooted close, holding her hand. "I'll make good on the promise. I participated in the contest because I wanted to. I fell for you that first night. But Devon got the drinks and your attention. I didn't."

Avienna's cheeks flushed pink.

"When you came into my shop, I took every opportunity I could to win you over. I thought if I could make an impression in the bedroom, that would set me apart, help seal the deal." Blake gazed out over the water. "I simply ran out of time. Your dad called, wanting his project a little sooner. I didn't have the chance to build another dancing pig." He squeezed Avienna's hand.

"When your dad announced the contest, I went for it, even though he'd kicked me out of the chance for a position in his company. Of course, Devon jumped at it too. I didn't care. My aim was to win you over. And then watching you with him . . ."

"Blake, the contest worked. I gave both of you an equal shot. That was my original intent. I didn't know who would volunteer, but I knew one thing. Anyone participating in a contest like that truly must want me. In the end, it all worked out."

"I do want you. Truly, I do." Blake said.

Avienna grinned. "You'll always be my number one. Truly."

"I'll be your number one if you be my princess."

"So what are you getting at?" she asked.

"Marry me. And I'm not playing games."

She nodded.

Blake leaned over and kissed her. "What kind of wedding do you want?"

"I want the same one like that girl had." Avienna laughed.

"That girl was Abby. You want one here?"

"Just like hers."

"We can do that. But there is one tiny favor I have to ask."

***

"Three weeks? Are you serious?" Lesander King's eyes widened with surprise. "That's not enough time to plan anything, let alone a wedding."

"Come on, dad, we can surely find people who can put something together. You've done it before." Avienna pleaded with her father.

"Not in three weeks." He scowled. "Why does the wedding have to be done in three weeks?"

"We can elope, if you wish, sir." Blake chimed in, hoping the older man agreed.

"Never. I'll not have my only daughter getting married without a proper ceremony, even if it's a small one." He shook his head. "What's the reason for such a rush?"

"Blake, do you want to tell him?" She smiled at her father. "You won't believe it when he tells you. I'm still wondering if I do."

Lesander King swiveled his leather office chair in Blake's direction. "I hope it's honorable, young man, or you'll be in huge trouble."

Blake grinned. "It's a little weird, but it's honorable enough, I suppose." He informed Mr. King about the promise he made Jared. "And in three weeks, my time is up."

The older man narrowed his eyes. "I hope you're not using my daughter for this and then plan on—"

"Don't even say that. How insulting." The sharp, incensed tone surprised Blake. He wasn't part of the family, yet, to speak in such a bold manner with its patriarch. Avienna's face flushed.

Instead Lesander King held Blake's gaze and leaned back in his chair. "Good. Good for you. Thank you for saying that." He leaned forward, topping Blake's hand with his. "I admire a strong man who can speak his mind, make his point, and show who's boss. I see a bit of fire in you."

"Thank you, sir. No matter what, I won't have my integrity questioned where Avienna's concerned. She stole my heart long before she even had a clue." He winked at the blushing girl next to him.

"Where are you from, son? Who is your father? You never told me his name."

Blake's pulse quickened. What would Lesander King say when he discovered his old business partner's son was about to become a son-in-law?

He pulled out the wallet and removed the pictures Jared had placed in the pockets. They remained there, a constant reminder of his origins, a life abandoned years ago.

Lesander King's face went pale. His eyes glittered with emotion. He opened his mouth, but no words came out.

"What's wrong, dad?" Avienna asked. She stepped behind the desk and stood beside her father.

"I'll be damned," the older man whispered. He kept staring at the pictures, flipping through them, studying each one. "You're Jared McCallahan's son?"

"I am, sir," said Blake, his voice barely above a whisper.

Avienna looked at both men, confused.

"I loved that man. One of the smartest business people I ever met. I've not yet found anyone who can match him still." Lesander King turned his gaze up at Blake. "We were best friends, Jared and I. Inseparable, almost. Our respect and trust for each other ran deep. We had a great business going. But one day, it all changed. Don't know what happened or why, but his interests started leaning toward a much different path than what we'd originally agreed on."

"And because of that, you sent him a letter to end the business relationship. You bought him out. I found the letter, sir." Blake stared down at the floor.

Mr. King's face softened like he was in a dream. "Broke my heart. There's been many a day I've thought about him, wanted him back, hoping we could work something out."

"If it makes you feel any better, sir, I walked away from the family business myself. I knew there were more honorable ways for making money. When I saw that letter, I wanted to find you more than anything."

Avienna's lip pulled into a bright smile. "And here we all are." She walked away from the desk and returned carrying a small bag. "You need to see this."

Lesander King watched with amusement while Avienna played the tin whistle. The little golden pig whirled, stood en pointe, and twirled to the piped music. She finished after several notes and laid the tin whistle on the desk. "What do you think about what Blake made for you?"

"That's the cutest thing I've ever seen." The older man laughed. "I think people will snatch these up. How did you come up with the idea?"

Blake thought fast. He couldn't tell King that Aaron had chipped in with the whistle. "When I was a kid, my grandmother told me a Danish fairytale about a swineherd who was given a magic flute by a troll. When the swineherd played the flute, the pigs danced." He chuckled. "I thought if I could capture that story in this figurine, I might have a winner."

"You've hit a home run. Creative too. Nothing like it out there." Lesander King patted Blake on the back. "I can see you'll be a chip off the old block, but better." He turned to Avienna. "As for you two, I'll make sure I find someone who can cater a reception as fast as you need them to."

"And the location will be at my place." Blake smiled.

***

Three weeks later, on the exact date ending the five-year stipulation, Hoot Owl Hollow hosted its second wedding. Blake stood before the minister, compliments of Abby's kind assistance in securing the one she'd used. Lesander King hired a top-notch catering company who set up everything, which included a pastry chef who created the most stunning, delicious cakes in all of the Southeast.

Guests included only close friends, family, and some of Lesander Kings most important business contacts. Calin and Aaron had been given the honor of sitting in the special place reserved for parents of the groom.

"He's about as close to a son as I'll ever have. We were real close. Worked together like a champion team," said Calin. He swiped away a stray tear slipping out of his eye.

"I hear you, neighbor. I think we did well with him. Finished making him what he is today." Aaron patted Calin's knee in agreement.

The violin and flute players started the processional music, and everyone paid close attention. The bridal party came forward, starting with Abby and Eric, followed by two pairs of Avienna's friends, ending with Devon escorting Cindy down the aisle once again. She briefly laid her head affectionately on Devon's shoulder as they walked. He acknowledged the gesture with a gentle squeeze of her arm.

When the bridal march played, Avienna walked down a grassy aisle tinged with the tops of wildflowers and rose petals. She wore a bridal crown that sparkled in the sun. On her hair, pearls and crystals glistened. Her dress created a fairy-like appearance, and Blake wondered if she truly wasn't a mere figment, a fairy princess stepping out of a story book, and once someone closed the book, she'd disappear forever.

When she placed her arm through his, Blake knew this wasn't a fiction story, but the final step in making his dream a reality. Avienna would be his. He thought about the golden box sitting beside the groom's cake, which held an edible gold-leaf pig on top. The mystery of the box ended today.

During the reception, Cindy came up to Blake. "Congratulations. I really mean it."

"Have you forgiven me at all?" Blake asked. They had kept their distance at Abby's reception.

"Yeah, I have." She nodded. Her face held a calm expression. "It was hard at first, but we have to be true to ourselves, even if it means the other one may hurt for a while." Cindy stared off into the crowd of guests. "That's just the way it goes."

"I know." Blake nodded and ate a bite of cake.

Cindy smiled to someone in the crowd. Blake followed her gaze and saw Devon coming their way. "Excuse me. Gotta run"

Blake watched Devon and Cindy smiling at each other and talking. She laughed when he whispered something in her ear. "I think there's something between those two," Blake murmured to himself.

"It's time to find out what's in that box." Avienna slipped up behind Blake and wrapped her arms around him.

"Just looking for the right time to get away."

"No time like the present." She picked up the box and handed it to Blake, kissing him on the lips. "Go look. This reception is not ending anytime soon."

He couldn't do what Avienna requested in the middle of a crowd of people. Clutching the box, he made a quick getaway to the cabin. Seated at his desk, Blake tugged on the top, hoping it might magically open. When that didn't work, he pulled out a letter opener. For several minutes he worked the tip into the lock, wiggling it back and forth. No amount of pressure or manipulation opened the box.

"Damn!" Blake sank back against his chair, defeated.

"You looking for this?" A male voice sounded from behind.

"What the hell?" Blake jumped out of his seat and stared straight into Shorty's face. A small key dangled from the man's fingers.

"Happy to see me?" Shorty smiled and hugged Blake like a long-lost brother. "Man, it's great to see you again. I've missed you, buddy."

"Doubt that. None of you bothered to call. In five whole years." Blake held up five fingers and frowned.

"We waited for you to call first, let us know you made it all right. When we didn't hear anything, we just thought you didn't like us anymore."

"Man, you're not right." Blake took the tiny key from Shorty. "Who told you to come here today?"

"Your dad. Told him I didn't give you lock-picking lessons because you high-tailed it out of town so fast. But it was Uncle Calin who first told us about your wedding." Shorty grinned. "That wife of yours is a looker. Much better than my aunt's cousin's niece."

"How come I never saw you?"

"Kept out of sight and sneaked in when you weren't looking. Told Uncle Calin to keep mum because it had to do with your future."

Blake turned to the box. "Now for the moment of truth. You know what's in here?"

"C'mon, man, you know your dad doesn't tell me everything." Shorty punched Blake softly on the arm.

The tiny key fit. One turn and the top opened.

Both men peered into the box. Nothing inside but a few sheets of paper with legalese writing. Blake opened up the first sheet and read:

Dear Son,

Congratulations on your wedding day. If you're reading this right now, it's because you've said your vows. I want to wish you every happiness in life. I've held back on the path to marriage, but I know the value of having a trusted, loyal partner on your side. The world being what it is, it's much easier with legalities when a legitimate union is involved.

I've made some unusual choices in life. I would have liked for you to have joined me, but I respect the right of a man to make his own way in the world when he wants to. Long ago I made some good money, just the way you dream of doing. I took those funds and did something special with them. If you go to the website shown at the end of this letter, you will see what I have given you for your inheritance. I've provided you the login name and password for your account. Please change the password after signing in.

If we don't ever see each other again, just know that I will always love you. You're a fine man, and you're my son. Times and circumstances change, but my concern for your well-being will stay the same with the passing of time.

Love,
Dad

Blake looked at Shorty.

"What are you waiting for? Log in, buddy." Shorty pulled the laptop open and motioned for Blake to find the website.

"Mind if I join you guys?" Lesander King walked toward the two men at the desk.

Shorty held out his hand and introduced himself.

"Jared couldn't come?" King asked Shorty.

"No sir. It's rather a private matter for him, and he doesn't discuss much along those lines with me."

"I told our good man here," said King, pointing to Blake, "that Jared was one of the finest in business I ever met. But you tell my old best friend that his son is about to out-do him."

Shorty smiled and replied, "Sir, just between us, you're getting the best one of the two. Trust me on that one. And you didn't hear it from me."

"Wow," Blake whispered. "Would you look at this." He moved away so the men could see the screen. The website showed an investment company, along with the account Jared mentioned in the letter.

"I'll be damned," said Lesander King. "That's a hell of a lot of money."

"Read this." Blake handed his father-in-law the letter.

"Unbelievable. He must have used the buy-out money I gave him." King handed the letter back to Blake.

Shorty said, "Looks like you're set, Blake. You'll have enough to keep you sitting pretty for life. You and that gorgeous wife of yours."

"He'll be doing better than that," said King, laughing. "Blake, I've decided that for right now, I'm adding you as half owner of my business empire. You and I will be the rulers of the roost. King & McCallahan, just like the way it was in the beginning. What do you think about that?"

"That's fantastic, sir." Blake wanted to shout for joy. Everything he'd wanted seemed to click for the first time.

"Well, gentlemen, it's been fun, but I gotta get back on the road." Shorty stepped toward the front door. Blake, anything you want me to tell your dad, Eileen, anyone?"

"Tell him that he got his wish. And when I'm ready, maybe someday I'll call him."

A perplexed look crossed Shorty's face.

"Sorry, dude, but I'm still sore at him for not even calling to check in. That really hurt my feelings. Tell him thank you for the inheritance. I'll follow the best of what he taught me and be a wise steward of it."

Shorty smiled. "You bet I'll tell him. And you and me, we're always good, I hope."

Blake walked over and hugged the man who'd always been there for him when his father wasn't. "We're always good, my friend. Take care."

Blake and Lesander King watch Shorty leave. Blake changed his password and logged out of the website.

"I think we have a reception to finish up," said King.

The men walked back to the crowd. Blake danced the evening away in Avienna's arms. Lesander King mingled with all the guests. Aaron and Calin took turns dancing with Abby and the other bridesmaids. Later that night Blake brought his bride back to his charming cabin where they made love now as husband and wife.

"I fell in love with this cute place the moment I saw it," said Avienna cuddling against Blake. "I pretend I'm in a fairy tale when I'm here."

Blake said nothing but kissed her lips.

A year later, Hoot Owl Hollow hosted its third wedding. Devon and Cindy said their vows by the river, just as Abby and Avienna had done before. There was a new person joining the guests. Little Saraya, Blake and Avienna's new addition to the family, cooed and clapped the moment the bridal couple said I do.

"She'll have her big moment someday." Blake looked over at his little girl and chucked her under the chin.

Avienna leaned over and kissed Blake. "Every day with you is my big moment."

END

About The Author:

Scarlet Darkwood wields a mighty pen, or at the very least, delivers mighty punches to the computer keys when she's typing furiously on a story. She likes dark and twisted, and the weirder, the better.

Always preferring Avant Garde themes, her stories take the reader on unusual adventures, exploring the darker parts of the human psyche as she whips out cunning prose wrapped in provocative themes. Sometimes she veers from her beaten path and takes a happy-go-lucky romp in the brighter sides of life, kicking up her style into sharp, snappy dialogue and clever descriptions.

Writing in several genres unleashes her imagination so she never grows bored. From a young age, she's enjoyed writing and keeping diaries, but didn't start creating novels until 2012. She's a Southern girl who lives in Tennessee and enjoys the beauty of the mountains. She lives in Nashville with her spouse and two rambunctious kitties.

For more information about the latest concerning Scarlet and her work, you can do the following:

Visit her BLOG at: www.scarletdarkwood.com
Follow her on Twitter at:
http://twitter.com/ScarletDarkwood
Follow her on Facebook:
http://www.facebook.com/scarletdarkwoodauthor

Check out Scarlet's other works:

Romance:
Escape from Purgatory
Words We Never Speak
Surya

Crime:
Death by Design

Erotic Romance:
Pleasure House
Dance of Desire
Taming Bad
Master of The House
Mistress of The House

Short Stories:
Hard Way In
Fun with Dick and Peter
Naughty and Nice
Tech Support
An Enchanting Hideaway
Three Card Spread
Castus Vindicta
Sweet Secrets